# MOONBATH
—
## Yanick Lahens

TRANSLATED FROM THE FRENCH BY
EMILY GOGOLAK

INTRODUCTION BY
RUSSELL BANKS

DEEP VELLUM PUBLISHING
DALLAS, TEXAS

Deep Vellum Publishing
3000 Commerce St., Dallas, Texas 75226
deepvellum.org · @deepvellum

Deep Vellum Publishing is a 501C3
nonprofit literary arts organization founded in 2013.

ISBN: 978-1-941920-56-6 (paperback) · 978-1-941920-57-2 (ebook)
LIBRARY OF CONGRESS CONTROL NUMBER: 2016959433
—

This work received the French Voices Award for excellence in publication and translation. French Voices is a program created and funded by the French Embassy in the United States and FACE (French American Cultural Exchange).

Cover design & typesetting by Anna Zylicz · annazylicz.com

Text set in Bembo, a typeface modeled on typefaces cut by Francesco Griffo for Aldo Manuzio's printing of *De Aetna* in 1495 in Venice.

Distributed by Consortium Book Sales & Distribution · (800) 283-3572 · cbsd.com

Printed in the United States of America on acid-free paper.

*International Praise for Yanick Lahens*

*Winner of the Prix Femina, 2014*
*Winner of a French Voices Award, 2015*

"Yanick Lahens adeptly dipped her pen nib in tears to write *Moonbath*. She brandished her writing instrument with dexterity, creating Cétoute as a metaphor symbolizing both the pain and the promise of Haiti."
—LANIE TANKARD, *The Woven Tale Press*

"Lahens is the most important living female Haitian author wrting in French."
—PROFESSOR CHRISTIANE MAKWARD, Pennsylvania State University review

"[Lahens] describes her country with a forceful beauty—the destruction that befell it, political opportunism, families torn apart, and the spellbinding words of Haitian farmers who solely rely on subterranean powers." —*Donyapress*

"One of the finest voices of Haitian contemporary literature." —*L'Ob's*

"Everything is there, the content, powerful, and the style, poetic." —*Les Echos*

"Its poetic and political reflections are a prosperity…"—*Feuilleton*

"Her work occupies a privileged place in the feminine literature in Haiti, by its independence of spirit and its freedom of tone."—*Les Francophonies*

"From the writing of Yanick Lahens we find in *Moonbath*, these spaces of 'faults.' Those moments when everything can tilt, where the encounter exists, where it arises chaos, tragedy, and Beauty. A perpetual questioning of the imaginary, the social constructs, their encounters with the Other, on the scale of men and women." —*Africultures Magazine*

"Her powerful magical words give this magisterial novel a violent beauty."
—NOELLA at *NOFI News*

"…luxurious and mixed language…" —Radio Télévision Luxembourg

"Yanick Lahens offers here a personal and contrasting picture of her country, with a complex and hallucinatory, lyrical and intimate narrative, inhabited by a powerful breath. The magic operates and one lets oneself bewitched."
—*Encres Vagabondes*

"The literature of Haiti, already so fertile, is being enriched with this book."
—*l'Humanite Daily News*

At the end of the work, the reader will find a genealogical tree and a glossary to provide the definition of the words followed by an asterisk upon their first occurrence.

> I am Atibon-Legba
> My hat comes from Guinée
> So does my bamboo cane
> So does my old pain
> So do my old bones [...]
> I am Legba-Bois Legba-Cayes
> I am Legba-Signangnon [...]
> I want yams to soothe my hunger
> Malangas and pumpkins
> Bananas and sweet potatoes
>
> RENÉ DEPESTRE
> *A Rainbow for the Christian West*

> [...] he destroyed this beauty that
> could have led me to fall into relapses
> of desire [...]; I resemble God's old
> mistress, Death.
>
> MARGUERITE YOURCENAR
> *Fires*

# INTRODUCTION

From the moment in 2014 when Yanick Lahens's novel *Bain de lune* was published in France and won the prestigious Prix Femina, I have wanted to read it. Haitian and French friends and fellow-writers were urgently recommending the book to me. But unfortunately my French is American schoolboy French and is incapable of registering literary quality or intent. In French, I could barely get the gist of the story and not much more. Now that I can read it in English, thanks to this excellent translation by Emily Gogolak, it's clear that I was wise to have waited, for *Moonbath* is a linguistically subtle, supremely intelligent work of art that both requires and abundantly rewards close attention from its reader. In this sense, and in many others as well, it compares favorably with Patrick Chamoiseau's *Texaco* and Toni Morrison's *Beloved*. The reader has to be able to hear the unique voice (I should say, the voices) of the novel in order to experience it.

In *Moonbath*, there are essentially two alternating, intercut voices, two distinct points of view. The first, set off in italics, is the voice of a woman whose name and identity and fate we won't fully learn until the end of the novel. Lyrical and mysterious, infused with lamentation, hers is a story of betrayal and abandonment and ultimate redemption. It is the spiritual center of the book.

The second is the collective, choral, female voice of a community—the point of view of a people as opposed to that of a person—and thus in an important sense it is the political center of the book. It drives the narrative, carrying us through generations from the pre-Duvalier era to the near present, in which everything changes and yet nothing changes. Taken together, the two voices weave a spiritual and political tapestry that is nothing less than the history of the Haitian people.

And yet, for all its Haitian particulars—the beliefs, ceremonies, and ancient traditions of *voudon*, the culture and language of an isolated Kreole hillside village, the lives and deaths of three generations of a large extended family—it is a universal story. What is true and inescapable for Lahens's characters is true and inescapable for all of us. And for all its references to the contemporary world—the American occupation(s) of Haiti, the reign of the Duvaliers and the *macoutes*, the rise and fall of Aristide, catastrophic hurricanes, the tragic drownings of migrants fleeing to Miami, even the recent United Nations-sponsored cholera epidemic—Lahens's story is as ancient and classical as Greek tragedy. It could have been set in hundreds, probably thousands, of places in the world, from the hills of Honduras to the Sudan to Cambodia. I can imagine this story being set in any isolated village anywhere, even in Maine or Mississippi or Idaho. It's set in Haiti only because that happens to be the world Yanick Lahens knows best.

A great novel changes its reader's imagination. We close the book with our vision of the world and humanity altered, revised in a deep and lasting way and not merely embellished. When we finish Morrison's *Beloved*, for example, we believe in the felt reality of what we experienced there: the inhuman closure of slavery, the necessary murder of a child in order to save it from a life worse than death, the loving ongoing presence of a ghost. That is the unique power of great fiction: it provides its reader with an experience, not just an account. *Moonbath* has the same effect. This is not "magic realism"—it is realism of the highest order. So that, by the time we come to the final pages, we have lived through everything that Lahens's characters have lived through, their sufferings and joys, their cruelties inflicted and received, their religious ecstasies and denials, and the ongoing presence of their gods. The reader who finishes this novel will be different than the reader who began it.

*Russell Banks*
July 2017

I.

*After a madness lasting three days, here I am, stretched out, at the feet of a man I don't know. My face a hairsbreadth from his worn, muddy shoes. My nose overtaken by a stench that nearly revolts me. To the point of making me forget this vise of pain around my neck, and the bruise between my thighs. Difficult to turn over. To stand back up. To put one foot on the ground before the other one follows. To cross the distance that separates me from Anse Bleue. If only I could escape. If only I could run as far as Anse Bleue. Not once would I return. Not a single time.*

*But I cannot. I can't anymore…*

*Something happened at dusk on the first day of the storm. Something that I still can't explain. Something that broke me.*

*Even though my eyes are closed, nearly shut, and my left cheek is pushed right up against the wet sand, I still manage, and this gives me some relief, to look over this village built like Anse Bleue. The same narrow huts. All the doors and all the windows shut. The same leprous walls. On both sides of the same muddy road leading to the sea.*

*I want to force a cry up from my belly to my throat and make it spurt out from my mouth. Loud and clear. Very loud and very clear until I rip these big dark clouds above my head. Crying for the Grand Maître,★*

7

Lasirenn,★ and all the saints. How I would love for Lasirenn to take me far, very far, on her long and silky hair, to rest my aching muscles, my open wounds, my skin all wrinkled by so much water and salt. But before she hears my calls, I can only pass the time. And nothing else…

All that I see.

All that I hear.

All that I smell.

Every thought, fleeting, full, overpowering. Until I understand what happened to me.

The stranger took out his cell phone from his right pocket: a cheap Nokia like the ones you see more and more at the All Stars Super-market in Baudelet. But he couldn't use it. His whole body trembled. So much that the phone flew out of his hands and fell straight on my left temple. A little more and the Nokia would have hit my eye…

The man backed away abruptly, his eyes terrified. Then, working up the courage, he bent over slowly and stretched out his arm. He grabbed the phone quickly while taking extraordinary care to not touch me.

I heard him repeat very quietly, three times in a row, his voice choked with emotion: "Lord have mercy, lord have mercy, lord have mercy." I still hear his voice…It gets mixed up with the sea that writhes in wild sprays upon my back.


In my head, the images rush. Clash. My memory is like those wreaths of seaweed detached from everything, dancing, panicking on the foam of the waves. I would like to be able to put these scattered pieces back together, to hang them up one by one and reconstruct everything. Everything. The past. The time from long ago, like yesterday. Like three days ago.

*Year after year.*
*Hour after hour.*
*Second by second.*

*To retrace in my mind the route of a schoolgirl. Without brambles, without bayahondes,\* without an airplane in the night sky, without fire. To retrace that route as far as the wind that, this night of the storm, enchants me, intoxicates me. And these hands that make me lose my footing. Stumble.*

*To piece together the whole sequence of my existence, to understand once and for all... To bring back to life, one by one, my grandfathers and my grandmothers, great-grandfathers and great-grandmothers, as far back as my franginen\* forefather, to Bonal Lafleur, to Tertulien Mésidor and Anastase, his father. To Ermancia, Orvil, and Olmène, who were like water and fire to each other. Olmène whose face I do not know. Olmène whom I always missed and whom I still miss.*

*What a storm! What a tumult! Throughout this story, it will be important to pay attention to the wind, the salt, the water, not just to men and women. The sand was turned around and upside-down in the greatest disorder. Like land waiting to be sowed. Loko\* blew for three days in a row and swallowed the sun. Three long days. The sky turned a lighter and lighter gray. Milky in places.*

*"Do not do what you might regret," my mother hammers into me. "Don't do it."*

*I ramble like an old woman. I rant like a mad woman. My voice breaks at the back of my throat. It's still because of the wind, the salt, the water.*

2.

The elusive gazes of the men, the slightly aghast looks from the women, upon the arrival of this rider, all to suggest that he was a dreadful and dreaded being. And it's true that we all dreaded Tertulien Mésidor.

Tertulien Mésidor loved to pass through all of the villages, even the most distant, to test his power. To measure the courage of men. To weigh the virtue of women. And to check the innocence of children.

He had emerged from the candy colored curtains of the *devant-jour*. At that hour when, behind the mountains, a bright pink rips through shreds of clouds to run flat out over the countryside. Sitting on his ash gray horse, he was dressed as usual in a stately straw hat, the wide brim turned down over two bulging eyes. A cutlass hung from his belt and following his lead were two other riders, who advanced with the same slow and resolute steps as their master. Tertulien Mésidor went toward the fish stall that reeked of offal and decomposing flesh. At his approach, we started talking very loudly. Much louder than usual, vaunting the variety of fish, the quality of the vegetables and provisions, but without taking our eyes off the rider. The more we watched him the louder we spoke. Our racket on this dawn was nothing but a mask, another, for our acute awareness. When his horse reared, the procession froze. Tertulien Mésidor bent down to whisper into the horse's ear and to caress its mane. "Otan, Otan," he murmured softly. The animal stomped in place and shook its tail. The man with the wide-brimmed hat wanted to go ahead on the rocky path between the stalls.

With a gesture of authority, he hit the flanks of the horse with his heels and, squeezing the bridle, forced the animal to trot in that direction.

He had hardly advanced a few meters when he took the reins to stop himself again. The movement was so abrupt that the two other riders had a hard time holding back their horses, who were also stomping now. Tertulien Mésidor had just glimpsed, sitting among all the women, Olmène Dorival, the daughter of Orvil Clémestal, whose smile split the day in two like the sun and who, without realizing it, had twisted the bottom of her skirt and slid it between her thighs. Two eyes were already undressing her and she didn't have the slightest suspicion of it.

By the light trembling of his nostrils, the two other riders knew what to expect. Tertulien Mésidor kept his eyes fixed for a few seconds on this band of fabric that hid Olmène Dorival's spring and flower. It took his breath away. For a few seconds. Just a few seconds. But long enough to lose himself. Captive to a magic spell with no explanation.

Tertulien Mésidor's desire for Olmène Dorival was immediate and brutal, and it sparked within him a longing for entangled legs, furtive fingers, hips taken right between his palms, the scent of ferns and wet grass.

Tertulien Mésidor must have been fifty-five. Olmène Dorival was barely sixteen.

He owned three quarters of the lands on the other side of the mountains. He was a *don*.★ A great *don*.

More often than not she went barefoot and the only shoes she had ever worn were hewn from rough leather.

He had made several trips to Port-au-Prince, and had even traveled beyond the seas and danced the *son*★ with the mulattoes of Havana.

She had only left the limits of Anse Bleue to accompany her mother to the fish market in Ti Pistache, which smelled of rot and offal, and where flies danced wild *sarabandes*. Or, recently, a little further away, to the big market in Baudelet.

Unverifiable legends and tenacious truths hatched under the name of Tertulien. They said that he had stolen, killed. That he'd had as many women as there were in our village of peasant women and fishermen. And many other things…

In the monotony of very ordinary days, Olmène Dorival only escaped by the graces of the gods, who sometimes straddled her in dreams, tempers, colors, and words.

3.

Tertulien, taking the reins of his beautiful ash-gray horse, leaned over to caress its mane again. But all of a sudden, not being able to stand it any longer, he clapped his hands in one quick, brusque motion, toward Olmène. The sound echoed in all of our ears like a whip. Olmène Dorival did not think the command was meant for her. Neither did we. She had, like all of us, sometimes noticed this rider in the dust of the streets or on the Frétillons' porch, next to the big general store, in Baudelet. But she had done nothing but notice him, with due distance. He belonged to the others— the victors, the rich, the conquerors—not to the conquered, the defeated, like her. Like us. Poor like salt, *maléré*, ill-fated.

Olmène turned around but all she saw behind her were Man Came the elderly medicinal herb vendor, Altéma the amputee sleeping right on the floor, and a young man holding a donkey's bridle. She understood that she alone had to face the gaze of this man, the mere mention of whom cast a dark shadow over the eyes of her father, Orvil Clémestal, and made his mouth swell with a dense saliva, which he spat out in a thick stream into the dust. She told herself that she would pretend to have seen nothing. Heard nothing. She lowered her head softly and pushed her disorderly braids back beneath her scarf. Then she played at arranging whatever fish—sardines, kingfish, parrot fish—her father and brother had caught the previous day, laying out the sweet potatoes, yuccas, red beans, and millet in the basket that she and Ermancia, her mother, had placed on the ground. Raising her head, she took a long look at the man on the horse. He started to want everything: her wrists, her mouth, her breasts, her flower, and her spring. And, while she scanned every trait of Tertulien Mésidor's face behind the smoky circles that rose from his pipe, Ermancia finished laying out everything she had brought with her daughter from her *jardin.* *

One of the two riders following Tertulien approached Olmène and pointed to his master. Tertulien took off his hat and, with a fixed grin that was at once a smile and a threat, asked Olmène to sell him some fish. He bought everything. He who, by several accounts, stopped eating fish long ago. Ever since a kingfish in quick-broth had nearly killed him some years earlier. But that day Tertulien would have bought anything and everything. That's what he did. He didn't haggle as he usually did over prices, and he paid the fisherman and farmers their due. He bought Ermancia's millet, sweet potatoes, red beans, and yuccas, which the two other riders hauled behind their horses.

Like all of us, Olmène had occasionally seen a truck, or some horses or donkeys, reeling under the weight of all sorts of goods, crossing the salty lands, forking behind the Mayonne River in the distance and climbing the bridge until disappearing in the direction of Tertulien Mésidor's silent estate. Like all of us, she imagined, without saying a word and with a mixture of curiosity and envy, what these cargoes could be hiding. Whatever she did or didn't know, it was beyond what she could possibly imagine. Beyond what we, too, could even dream up. And if a smile twisted our lips or exposed our toothless gums in those moments, it was impossible, for her and us alike, to not blame the world for just a few seconds. To not blame those who resemble us as two drops of water do each other, to not take it out on the Mésidors and their kind. The maids, who once a week braved the trip to the market in Ti Pistache, Roseaux, or Baudelet, sometimes said things that piqued our curiosity for that world. A world that we, the men and women of Anse Bleue and all the surrounding towns and villages, nonetheless avoided. With a determination matching that with which the Mésidors kept us at a distance.

A game that chained us all to the Mésidors and that shackled them to us despite themselves. A game that we, victors and captives, had mastered long ago. Very long ago.

An ancient story entangled the Mésidors, the wind, the earth, the water, and us. But this is not some story about the origins of the world or the mists of time.

Just a story about men when the gods had just barely stepped away…

When the sea and the wind still hissed in whispers or wailed their names of foam, fire, and dust at the top of their lungs. When the waters traced a straight line at the edge of the sky and blinded us with the blueish glow. And when the sun levitated like a gift or crushed like destiny.

A story of tumults and very ordinary events. Sometimes of furors and hungers. At times, of blood and silence.

And sometimes of pure joy. So pure…

A story where a new world already straddles the old one. In fits and starts, like you might say about the gods when they straddle a *chrétien-vivant*…★

Such it was that, on this dawning day in Ti Pistache, not far from Anse Bleue, a village of rock, salt, and water nestled at the feet of the high mountains of Haiti, Tertulien Mésidor, master of his estate, was shaken to his core by the sight of Olmène Dorival, the peasant girl nonchalantly crouched on her heels, facing a basket of fish, vegetables, and provisions at a distant market in the countryside.

4.

The Mésidors, due east, on the other side of the mountains towering over Anse Bleue, had always coveted land, women, and goods. The family's destiny had crossed that of the Lafleurs and their descendants, the Clémestals and the Dorivals, forty years earlier. That day in 1920, when Anastase Mésidor, Tertulien Mésidor's father, had stripped Bonal Lafleur, Olmène Dorival's great-great-grandfather, of the last *carreaux*★ of his *habitation,*★

where *acajous* and *mombins*, the coffee of the maquis, still grew under the shade of elms. Bonal Lafleur got this property from his mother, who wasn't from the village of Anse Bleue but from Nan Campêche, in the mountains sixty kilometers south.

Anastase Mésidor had already seized the best lands of the plateau. But he also eyed others to sell for the price of gold to explorers and mavericks who came from afar, like those in the United West Indies Corporation, who had descended upon the island with the arrival of the Marines. Persuaded that they were like the *fincas* of Santo Domingo or the *haciendas* of Cuba, great properties that would make them rich and, at the same time, would transform us at last into civilized peasants: Christians, wearing shoes, hair clean and combed. Tamed but landless. "Never," a word that Solanèle Lafleur, Bonal's mother, had repeated dozens of times to her son while tracing a cross on the ground and pointing, quickly and with outspread arms, to the steep slopes of the mountains. There up high, in the *dokos*,★ where the spirit of the *Ancêtres marrons*★ still blew. "The land, my son, it's your blood, your flesh, your bones, you hear me!" Anastase Mésidor had put a curse on the Roseaux brothers, Pauléus and Clévil, who thought they could stand up to him and play the rebels. They disappeared in the fog of the first hours of the day, on the road that led to their *jardin*. One was found on the Peletier Morne, hanging like a rag doll from a mango tree, and the other was devoured by swine on the side of the road leading from Ti Pistache to the village of Roseaux.

We, the Lafleurs, had the reputation of being unbreakable and the bearers of powerful, even fearsome, *points.*★ For kilometers and kilometers, many thought this power extraordinary and envied it.

An unshakable power. Yet this solid reputation couldn't stand up to Anastase Mésidor's insistent offer: one morning, grinding his teeth before a surveyor in a black wool hat and a notary in a dark gray three-piece suit that was much too small on him, Bonal Lafleur was forced to give up his lands.

After a script that started with the words "Liberty, equality, fraternity, the Republic of Haiti" and ended with "here collated," Anastase Mésidor, the notary, and the surveyor made it clear to Bonal that he was no longer the proprietor.

His thumb smeared with ink barely stuck on the paper in the guise of a signature, Bonal Lafleur demanded his due from Anastase Mésidor. He had nonetheless sold him, with a heavy heart, some of the most beautiful of the lands of the Lafleur heirs, in the wide fertile plains surrounded by the mountains that rose southward over Anse Bleue. The mountains with slopes still green, very green, even if some fine strands of white already streaked their thick hair.

Anastase Mésidor, to Bonal's immense surprise, paid in cash, a big smile on his lips. A meager sum that Bonal had to share with a cohort of claimants whose rights to the land were far from clear. In looking at his ink-stained thumb, Bonal remembered contentions with a long list of brothers and sisters, cousins, from a first marriage, a second, a third, and others. Without forgetting all those who wouldn't fail to emerge from the surrounding lands with the announcement of this sale. One day, he had wanted to stop counting the interested parties, after a fight between the rival branches had nearly ended in blood drawn by machetes. Each recalling, with the sharp edge of their blade, events that had fixed borders and bounds. Even if Bonal had tried to stop counting, the fragmentation of the land hadn't stopped. Upon leaving the notary's office, Bonal, remembering the incident, shook his head from right to left under his floppy straw hat, frayed on the sides, while touching the bills in his right pocket.

All these memories came to weave a web of dark paths in his head, leading nowhere. A light vertigo came over him. And then, above all, there was Anastase Mésidor's smile. Not clear. Too good to be true. A smile that sent a chill down his spine. A smile that was a sign of nothing good to come. He thought for a moment of the Grand Maître high above, sighing, his throat dry. But God, the Grand Maître, was really too far to quench his thirst, and Bonal, touching the bills again, settled on some good glassfuls of *clairin*.★ Not one of those *trempés*★ with macerated herbs, spices, and bark. No. A good *clairin*, pure, to scald his tongue, burn his throat, and never says and wake his soul up in the middle of beautiful flames so that, for just a few hours, his life appeared before him like a luminous road without brambles. Without thickets. Without *bayahondes*. Without Anastase Mésidor. Without a cumbersome family. Agile on his legs with their protruding muscles, chin slightly forward, he advanced with a resolute stride in the direction of Baudelet.

"So many offspring for all these men! So many! Ten, fifteen, twenty, and even more!" sighed Bonal. Nonetheless, this idea of staying flush to the grave reinvigorated him, and he had a sweet and fleeting thought for a young *femme-jardin*★ from Nan Campêche, hard working, soothing, with strong thighs, and who had given him two children. He smiled as he lightly passed his hand over his thick beard and quickened his step, running after visions, despite the yaws that bit at his left heel.

But, in fear of being beaten up by the Marines and forced into one of their dreadful chain gangs or, worse, to be slaughtered with no warning just for being mistaken as one of the *cacos*★ rebels, Bonal changed his mind. Fear in his core, but agile like a wild cat, he preferred to use the steep paths. This fear twisted his guts, which he had to tame, to calm, he knew it all too well. Acid and painful fear. Fear that never loosened its grip. Stuck to us like a second skin. Planted inside us like a heart. Fear, a heart in itself. Beside you to love, share, laugh, cry, or get angry. So, in big strides, Bonal chose to move toward it in solitude. In the bushes and the *bayahondes*. To advance into the unknown. There where nobody came to look for us. Where the shadows are: in the eyes of beasts, under the bark of trees, in the sighs of the wind, under the leaves, in the stone beneath the dirt. He touched the small blister under his left arm and walked in this strange light of the undergrowth. Where he could merge with breath, the murmur of elements. Where he could be everything and nothing at once. There where Gran Bwa★ watches over his children and topples their fear. Where he reduces it to silence. Bonal hummed quietly, several times in a row, without even noticing it:

> *Gran Bwa o sa w té di m nan ?*
> *Mèt Gran Bwa koté ou yé ?*
> Gran Bwa what did you tell me?
> Grand Bwa where are you?

And went on with a light step, very light…

5.

Once he was on the path in Baudelet, Bonal slowed down in order to not arouse any suspicion and put on a normal face, the face of the villages, the face of a peasant smiling ear to ear, dazed by hunger and obscure divinities. Who says nothing, sees nothing, laughs, and never says no.

Bonal stopped, like on all the rare occasions when he went to Baudelet, at Frétillon's store, not far from the market. "The Haitian peasant is a child, I tell you all, a child!" Albert Frétillon liked to repeat as he twirled his thick mustache. And we always agreed, nodding our heads and staring at the ground. Which reassured Albert Frétillon, who stuck his thumbs underneath his suspenders and, to better observe us from above, lifted his head, stretched out his neck, and adjusted his glasses.

Frétillon's two sons, François and Lucien, and their only sister, Églantine, donning gloves and a hat, had gone to France on one of the large ocean liners that often docked in Badaulet to make a fortune in ports on both sides of the Atlantic. Albert Frétillon's fortune went back two generations, since an ancestor from La Rochelle had settled in Baudelet and started a lineage of mulattoes in this port town, the bourgeois of the province. In addition to his coffee trade, Albert Frétillon prepared, in a *guildive*★ at the entrance of the town, the best *clairin* around. Once the brandy was distilled, he spent most of his time on the porch of his house, next to the shop his wife ran. The chief of police, town judge, and director of Baudelet's only school met there, with some others, to bicker and speak their minds.

That afternoon, Anastase Mésidor, after purchasing Bonal's lands, joined them in their heated ranting. They hadn't let go of the events of the past few months. The director of the school in Baudelet brought up, once again, the cities bombed by the American Air Force, the bloody debacle of the leaders: Charlemagne Péralte assassinated, tied up naked to a wooden door and displayed in a public square; and Benoît Batraville, killed some months later. The volume rose. Some of them, like the judge, spoke of their sense of honor, pounding their chests as they went on, of an unbounded love for their homeland. Some of the others, like the chief of police and Anastase Mésidor, vaunted the benefits of this civilizing presence that was finally going to put an end to the fratricidal fights of the savages we were. "Yes, all, we are savages!" In saying the word "savage," Anastase noticed Bonal standing in front of the store and beckoned him with his finger, with an insistence that didn't reassure the latter. Albert Frétillon had acquiesced to all of these opinions. Absolutely. The future and prosperity of his business depended on this total absence of opinion, on this conviction that had been planted in him, that we the peasants would never grow up.

Bonal took off his old straw hat and flashed them his biggest smile. He even let himself, as usual, be lulled to the point of vertigo by the subjunctive imperfects and Latin words of these gentlemen—a feeling he'd felt since leaving the notary's study—and he felt a strange premonition that confirmed this finger pointed at him. Then, addressing this unease, he decided to drown it in the *clairin* he was dreaming of since the sale of the lands. A real *clairin*.

At the first sip, just outside of Baudelet, Bonal naturally remembered the offering to make to Legba,★ to open the door to family divinities, the offering to Agwé,★ so that the ocean would keep feeding them for a long time, and to Zaka,★ so that the *jardins* would be more generous. The earth already seemed lighter to him, suggesting that the sun at its zenith had made a clean world, clear, emptied. He went hurriedly toward the bush, in the direction of Anse Bleue.

Bonal disappeared that same day. Without Zaka, without Agwé, without Legba. Those among us who didn't want to stand up to the powerful said that drunkenness was the cause of his inexplicable disappearance. Some swore having seen a group of men, riding donkeys, who had, without a doubt, taken Bonal's money and, then, his life. Others recalled the presence of a goat that stood on the edge of the road and spoke clearly, showing two golden teeth. Some swore they had seen an old woman who, after moving with the light step of young girl, must have disappeared in the gorge at the bottom of the ravine. The whole affair unfolding before the indifferent eyes of two Marines, each with an imposing gun slung over his shoulder.

And each of us added a little more, added a little more…

Trying to clear up all suspicion, Anastase Mésidor sent a messenger by horse to meet Dieula Clémestal, the mother of Bonal's four children: Orvil, Philogène, Nélius, and Ilménèse. But the anger had already shut Dieula's jaw shut to the point that she didn't say a word. Not a single word the whole time the messenger stood before her at the entrance to her hut, awkwardly fidgeting with the hat in his hands.

"Your honor, Madame Bonal! It's Anastase Mésidor who sends me to tell to you…"

In response, Dieula slowly lit her pipe. Very slowly. Exhaling strongly three times in a row without ever raising her head. Then she spat so loudly and so forcefully that the man left immediately. He did not even dare to turn around before disappearing on his horse at the end of the path.

This scene, as Orvil, Olmène's father, would often have to repeat later, left him with the first strong and indelible impression of what he was and what this messenger represented. Of who was big and who was not. Who was strong and who was weak. Of the hunter and the prey. Of who charges and who is trampled. Orvil Clémestal was just twelve years old. He and his younger sister Ilménèse hid in the folds of his mother's skirt.

That night, Bonal appeared to Dieula in a dream—"Like I see you here," she told her children and all of us. And Bonal had told her everything. Absolutely everything: the sale of the lands, the hidden paths to Baudelet, the finger pointed at him, buying the *clairin*, and, on the road, a sharp pain in his back. Inflicted by the point of a cutlass. And then nothing. Nothing more.

The next day, with Orvil, her oldest son, she went at dawn, without the slightest hesitation, to the exact place where Bonal's body was found: at the bottom of a ravine, in the middle of the brambles and *bayahondes*. Bonal's pockets were empty and a cloud of flies was swirling around his body, which was starting to swell. We were stunned, shocked, but not the least bit surprised. Dieula only reminded us of the power of dreams, the strength and the solidity of the threads that tied us to the Invisibles. We cried out

our pain, and then we silenced ourselves. Returning to our pla-
cidity. To our place. To our peasant silence.

Bonal's service had no drums. No wailing. Tears were swallowed.
No cries pulled up from the insides of women. No open remi-
niscing on the life of the deceased. Just the moaning and murmuring among the jerky sway of bodies back and forth. The
priests, gendarmes, and Marines knew nothing of it. A lugubrious and sad service whose only sound was the *asson,*★ the
prayers, the grief, the songs cornered between throat and mouth.
Despite the three sacred words murmured into Bonal's ear and
all of Dieula's skill, the celebrated *mambo,*★ the deceased didn't
designate anyone among us to welcome his *met-tet*★ and look
after our heritage and our blood. The *désounin*★ had failed, and
Bonal left carrying his Spirits with him. Those who led him,
led his house and protected the *lakou.*★ And we were not sure
that he had heard all of our messages to our Dead, to our *lwas*★
and all our Invisibles. So we all were afraid for the protection and life of the *lakou.*★ We were afraid for each one of us.

Once Bonal was buried not far from his house, Dieula called
all her Invisibles for a whole day and night. All of them. Her gods
and her Spirits. Her Invisibles from the paternal side and those
from her maternal side. The brave, the magnetic, the wise, the
compassionate, the powerful Ogou Kolokosso, Marinette Pyé-
-Chèch, Grann Batala Méji, Bossou Trois Cornes, Ti-Jean Pétro,
Erzuli Dantò, and all the others…

Two days later, her low chair at the door to her hut, Dieula started
to sing a strange psalm that seemed to come from afar. Not from
her insides but from further away. From the very heart of the earth.

And it climbed up her legs, into her organs. And from her throat it came out like a thread through a needle until it went beyond the heavens. Not one of us dared to bother her, out of fear of breaking this thread. She sang without ever stopping:

> *Yo ban mwen kou a*
> *Kou a fè mwen mal o !*
> *M ap paré tann yo*
> They hit me
> The blows hurt me very badly!
> I wait for them at the bend

And then, slowly, Dieula got up, put on a rough blue cotton dress, tied a red handkerchief around her head and another around her waist, where she buried an enameled goblet, half of a small empty calabash, and a bag holding her pipe and a little tobacco. She summoned Orvil, her older son, and told him what she had to do and that she would return soon. We saw her disappear on the other side of the Peletier Morne. Without a cent, without bread, without water, she walked in the thickets, the *bayahondes*, and the bushes, begging for food and shelter, to do penance and plead to her divinities to respond.

Dieula returned the afternoon of the eve of the storm, beneath a wall of menacing clouds. She did not want to be carried away by the powerful current of the Mayonne River, she told us. The penance had lasted a whole month. As proof, her feet were badly beat up and pain radiated from her lower back. Seeing her return, we cried out, wept, and danced. We had all been waiting—at once confident and worried. Dieula was exhausted, but her eyes were clear like the sky after rain. As though in all the time we hadn't seen her, her eyes had been soaked in light. Or fire. Or Gods.

She sat down with difficulty on her low straw chair at the entrance to her hut, her bloody and blistered feet in sandals whose thin leather had been marred by the dust of the trails and the water of the rivers and streams. She took off her shoes and asked Orvil to draw a tub of water so that she could soothe her feet, then asked for something to eat and drink. She swallowed a plateful of corn with black beans and *bananes musquées,* Orvil and Philogène standing behind her, and the two little ones at her sides.

Four days after her return, Anastase Mésidor's fourth son, who was born two years after Tertulien, died unexpectedly. Typhoid? Poisoning? Meningitis? The Mésidors never knew. We, in Anse Bleue, Ti Pistache, and Roseaux, without saying a word, believed beyond the shadow of a doubt…and we believe it still, that Dieula Clémestal had taken death by the hand and led it dutifully to the Mésidors' front door.

After the death of Bonal, who was then our *danti,*★ the life of the *lakou* was marked by prudence and vigilance. We had been hobbled, and we were afraid of falling until the day Bonal appeared in a dream to his brother, Présumé Lafleur. The latter gathered everyone in the early morning at the entry of his hut to tell us of the strange dream: "I saw Bonal walking toward me, as straight as an arrow. Dieula walked behind him but it was like she had shrunk, and it was Orvil, with his broad chest, who led them both." As Présumé Lafleur told his dream, tears rolled down Dieula's cheeks. She was relieved and pleased. Présumé went on: "I stood there, frozen, shocked.

And, just when I lifted a foot to walk toward my brother, he disappeared over the water as he pointed his finger to Orvil. And Dieula wept, wept, like she is weeping here before us." We all took Présumé at his word and we bowed to Bonal's will to make Orvil his successor, and the new *danti* of the *lakou*.

Dieula made some offerings to the divinities, waiting for Orvil to pass through all the steps of his initiation before he took *asson*. That ended a few weeks before his brother Philogène left for Cuba, a year before Dieula died, and three months after the Americans departed the island.

Orvil became our *danti* and oversaw everything, the fishing, the work in the *jardins*, the punishments, the offerings to the divinities, our protection against those more powerful than us—like the Mésidors, Frétillons, the chief of police. Our protection against all who resemble us as two drops of water do each other, but who were not us. Who were not from the *lakou*. He made sure that ambition never nested in any of the hearts of the *lakou*. None. We were branches of the same tree, arms from the same trunk, and we had to stay there.

But Orvil, though he was our *danti*, couldn't do anything to treat the underlying wounds, from which the blood of the earth gushed. The primal scars that dug into the sides of the hills. The rivers that shriveled and shriveled, bleeding out. The earth and rocks that kept piling up at the feet of the slopes when we pushed them away. The growing power of the hurricanes. The droughts, each one more devastating than the previous. Against those who left, detached themselves from the tree for a reason that was not ambition but looked a lot like it.

Orvil was powerless against these events that only seemed to want to follow, straight, straight ahead, a one-way road with no escape from fate.

6.

Nothing upset Olmène more than these acts of hate, tears, and blood between the Lafleurs and the Mésidors. Orvil, her father, sometimes relived them as though they had taken place the day before and not forty years earlier. Yet nothing troubled her as much in this dawn as the look of the lord and thug Tertulien Mésidor. A wind coming from the mountains stirred up the waves. Olmène looked at the sea, which seemed to breathe like a beast stretched out on its back, agitated by the ebb and flow of the blood of all the creatures and souls living within it. *Nan zilé anba dlo*, on the island under the waters. She secretly greeted the Dead, the Ancestors, and the Mysteries. Undoubtedly, Tertulien Mésidor's fleeting and flagrant presence had plunged her into a strange disorder. Strange, but good…We, too, were troubled by that brisk and bizarre visit, but we left Olmène to herself…To taste her first feelings as a woman.

It was said that Tertulien Mésidor got his power and his money from a pact with the devil. That in the right pocket of his pants he hid a free pass, in indelible ink, issued by one of the secret societies, Zobop, Vlingbinding, or Bizango, that surprised the innocent on the roads at night. That he even reigned over one of them as emperor. That in the room upstairs, at the back of the far south end, behind two doors that were always closed, he hid a hideous creature with two horns on its head and a cork-screw tail. Without ever having seen it, several among us swore to have heard it howl at the full moon. Regarding the death of his fourth son, Candelon, we heard that he had offered him up in exchange for richness and power to a blood-thirsty God, Linglinsou or Bossou Trois Cornes.

"But they say so many things," Olmène thought. She pushed back the blood that rose to her face and, with that blood, all these things said over and over again, endlessly repeated and rehashed, leaving the shock to fold into itself, inside of her, like an August storm.

As with God, if we believed in Tertulien, his power fascinated us all in spite of ourselves. Despite the suffering that he inflicted upon us, he fascinated us. Like his father, Anastase Mésidor, had fascinated us. Despite the wounds, thirst, pain, and hunger. And, since God made the earth tremble, overwhelmed the waters and crumbled the mountains, Tertulien perhaps had set his mind on resembling God. Maybe he wanted to outdo him by even making the stars and stones bleed. He was surrounded by this aura that power bestowed upon the strongest and that so often made us, the conquered, lower our heads and, nose to the earth, inhale the darkness.

When, some years before his death, a dispute had pitted his father, Anastase Mésidor, against men from the big city, the residents of these five hamlets and surrounding villages, including Anse Bleue, had armed themselves with machetes, cutlasses, and *bâtons gaïacs.*★ And, with the help of some *clairin*, they pushed back the assault. The Mésidors had been dealt an attack by conquerers coming from afar, and we had all felt insulted by it. All of us. Without exception. Go figure! But that's how we are.

This pitched battle, which threw back the assailants, sealed a strange pact, another one, between the Mésidors, Anse Bleue, Ti Pistache, Morne Lavandou, Pointe Sable, and Roseaux. As fearsome and cruel as they were, the Mésidors were ours. We were even proud of them. But make no mistake about it. Under the shared blow, under the whipped pride, mistrust and fear were sleeping. They were always there. They blew inland like a soft black wind, sweeping the grass of the hills, passing through souls, and descending the dry slopes until reaching the sea. And returning to the hills and descending again. For us, mistrust and fear of a new and unexpected cruelty on the part of the Mésidors. And for the Mésidors, mistrust and fear of our unpredictable vengeance. Who knows?

When Tertulien Mésidor returned home after his trip to the market in Ti Pistache that morning, he, unlike other days, thought neither of his business nor of his political contacts, let alone of his wife, Marie-Elda. The image of Olmène had already taken hold over his entire body and swept everything else away. Absolutely everything. A man's desire sharpened inside of him, and it made his eyes shine in the hot light of that early afternoon. He barely tasted what the servants put out for him on the table and he didn't even notice his wife's presence. "That's enough, I'm not hungry anymore. I already ate." At this very moment, all Tertulien Mésidor wanted a very young woman. Just one. A peasant, as he liked them. And not a meal.

It is the look of this man that Olmène had borne at the market in Ti Pistache. She had kept her eyes raised for a long time, but eventually dropped them before this rider who could have been her father and who had taken off his hat to talk to her, the daughter of a fisherman and a peasant. She had found the high and serene brow of man who, contrary to legends, contrary to what all of Anse Bleue slurred between clenched teeth, seemed to have a calm presence. The same calm with which he had gone inland toward his grand house with its big gates and all of its servants.

Ermancia, like the other women at market, like all of us, was caught between fear and wonder. Wonder sparked by the attention of a man that powerful, and fear by the often harmful consequences of such power over our lives.

7.

*The first moment of stupor over, the man whom I do not know, after having retreated, advanced toward me again. He leaned over again, his eyes wide open. And I saw his face twist slowly in a strange grimace, his jaw slacken, his mouth open as his lips trembled. That's when, all of a sudden, this face curled in on itself and the man started to cry out, with all of the force of his lungs, names that I didn't know:* "Estinvil, Istania, Ménélas, anmwé, osékou, *come to me, help me.*" *At times he screamed words that fear broke, stretched out, distorted, mixed up. It was like a seawall had given way. And he could no longer stop the waves that gushed from his mouth.*

*I, I wanted to ask him to stop. Tell him that I would explain. And since I couldn't, of course he continued to scream even more. It was awful!*

*Then, like he was mustering up the courage, he came even closer to me, his head bent forward, and opened wide his toothless mouth.*

No way to withdraw from nor escape his breath of night. No way. A breath to turn your stomach.

Wanting to drown myself in sleep. Just for a few minutes. Knees against my chin. Eyes shut. Shut inside of sleep like the inside of an egg. Let the night glide over my skin. With the memory of the coldness of the moon. Of the rippling water that sparkled like sequins.

At the edge of the village, a rooster shouts at the top of his lungs. Another responds to him. Both call forth a day that struggles to make itself seen.

"Do not do what you might regret," my mother hammered. "Do not do it!"


My blood throbs outside of me in this wind where I hear this muffled breathing, the clinking of a buckle unfastening...And the cold member, straight as a stick...My neck hits the sand. The tearing. My body is lifted off the ground. The pain around my neck...And then the night... the sea...Again the night. Liquid. Black.

No matter what, in this story, you have to pay attention to the wind, its saline breath on our lips, the moon, the sea, Olmène absent...The earth that doesn't give anymore. The stingy sea. And the foreigners arriving with their faraway customs. Their habits, their American cigarettes, their bodies, their odors, and their shoes that catch our eyes.

And I, who didn't want to be here anymore, here I am powdered with sand, crowned with seaweed and longing for Anse Bleue.

"Osékou, anmwé." There now, the cries of the stranger strike strong in my chest. Mixed up uncannily with my brother's cries from three days ago, in the night.

*My brother stops on each of the syllables of my name. He had to put his hands up to his mouth like a megaphone to make them travel. Far, very far. And then the cries of others who with him brave the night, the wind, the water to cry out my name. "Koté ou yé? Where are you? Answer!"*

*The people of Anse Bleue swam through the night and the water, their eyes open, like whales.*

8.

Even though there didn't remain much for them to sell—Tertulien Mésidor having bought so much from them in the early hours of the morning—Olmène and Ermanica decided to meet the other women at the market in Baudelet, which was bigger and busier than the one in Ti Pistache. The heat was already hanging over the paths leading to the Peletier Morne, weighing down the *chrétiens-vivants*, animals, and plants. Even the rocks groaned. Yet nothing slowed their course on those paths, cleared by bare hands, hard and polished like brick by the sun and the wind.

On market days, Olmène felt the weight of fatigue more strongly, having gotten up ahead of dawn with the children of the *lakou*, then climbed and descended the hill, a calabash on her head, another in her hand, in the search of water. But she had already forgotten her painful legs, her bruised feet, and walked straight as an arrow behind Ermanica. She sped up as she went inland toward the towns, leaving the sea to languish in her wake. That world spread out behind her, that great liquid country, could still, at any moment, swallow her in its immense, silent, beastly belly.

At times herbal, clear and so reassuring, the world she went toward could also, with no warning, turn her around, freeze her, and knock her over with its cascades of water, its storms, and its cliffs. These worlds had already taken a father, a cousin, a brother, or an uncle from us. Between the first break of light of the *devant-jour* and the sudden shadows of the afternoon, Olmène put one foot in front of the other, agile and quiet, into the arrogance, extravagance, and power of these worlds.

The trip seemed longer that day to Olmène, because of the silence of her mother, who never mentioned Tertulien Mésidor's insistence on buying their goods. Ermancia had seen nothing. Heard nothing. Olmène let herself slip into this same ring of silence, following her mother's lead. Yet Ermanica couldn't stop herself from thinking of Tertulien Mésidor, who resembled, as two drops of water do each other, his father, Anastase Mésidor, who unceremoniously and without restraint, at the mercy of his will, had taken so many women that he'd forgotten their names as soon as he'd had them. Scattering kilometers of the coast, the surrounding mountains, with children whose first names he didn't know, whose faces he didn't recognize. Even the women who were spared his monstrous lust, if they crossed themselves after passing him, it was because they were intrigued by all that power. Olmène and Ermancia had been, too, that morning.

They climbed the mountain, hardly feeling the rough limestone bruise the soles of their feet, cut their heels. Olmène eventually forgot the pain, her mother having told her so many times that feet unable to face the stones and rocks were useless, good for nothing: "God gave you feet so that you could use them!" They left very late that day and sped up their steps so as not to be surprised by too strong a sun. It was already almost unbearable because of the glare spreading out from the sea. As far as the eye could see. It gave off light as though condemning the earth to fire.

At the first turn at the top of the hill, Olmène traced the first dark green trees, which didn't grow thick but still escaped the vicious dryness of Anse Bleue. Entering Roseaux, she and Ermancia took a break, time to wipe their faces, relieve their bladders, to pick strands of *mangue fil* and stick them between their teeth. Time also to chat for a few minutes in front of Madame Yvenot's stand, and she offered them half of an avocado and a *kasav**. Olmène couldn't keep herself from looking at Madame Yvenot's new shoes, black with a buckle on the side. For the last two months she'd been dreaming of them.

Madame Yvenot, recently returned from the Dominican Republic, showed off her profits from selling provisions and *pois Congo*. What Ermanica knew of the Dominican Republic had started over meals shared with Josephina, a friend of her mother's from Duverger, back when there was trade with Pedro, Rafael, and Julio in Bani; it stopped with a death, blood, a scar on her left forearm, and a missing front tooth. She escaped Trujillo's massacre because her mother covered her up with her body and breathed her last breaths beneath the repeated strikes of the machetes and the heinous sound of the voices that cried: "*Malditos Hatianos, malditos.*" The events that sometimes disfigured her joys or filled her sleepless nights despite the fatigue of the days. Ermancia didn't even want to say the name of that part of the island, and settled on listening to Madame Yvenot in silence.

Changing the subject, her eyes insinuating, serpentine, she asked them why they were late. There's nothing to quicken the pulse of the slanderous, *mal parlante* Madame Yvenot more than taking out peoples' dirty laundry and wallowing in the salt of their tears, the red of their blood, the stickiness of their seed. And sniffing around, celebrating the odor of misfortune. Ermancia told her that Orvil had trouble getting up that morning because of the pain in his back. Madame Yvenot, pleased by this display of confidence, reminded her that she would wind up killing her old man of a husband: "You are going to finish him off, Ermancia!" They both laughed out loud. Ermancia started to tell the story of a woman whom she knew in her hometown and who, one day... She whispered the rest into Madame Yvenot's ear. And, when they laughed again, Olmène laughed with them, not because of their words, which had been muffled and which she didn't fully hear, but because of Madame Yvenot's enormous breasts, which shook all around like two wild horses each time she burst out laughing. That didn't make her forget Ermancia's lie, and it only further sharpened her curiosity for this older man who emerged from the fog and who had the power to make her mother lie.

At the market in Baudelet, they sat in their usual spot, under the leaves of one of the rare acacias that stood in the vast space where they exchanged what the lands gave them: mangos, avocados, bananas, plantains, sweet potatoes, breadfruit, greens, millet, and corn—with what the city offered—matches, thick blue cotton, soap, enameled utensils. This corner where she sat with her daughter, Ermancia had won it at the end of a fierce fight. She took hold of it the day after Grann Méphise, an elderly vendor who had taken her under her wing, died without leaving behind a daughter or a niece or a goddaughter to pass it down to. Another crass woman set up her stakes just after her death, while everyone was still in mourning. Ermancia stood before her, hands on hips, her skirt slightly hiked up on one side, and challenged her: "You stay in this place one second longer and I can no longer be held responsible for my actions!" After the usual cursing, the two women were held back from coming to blows, and the dispute was resolved by an improvised tribunal that immediately recognized Ermancia's right to the spot.

Olmène liked this stubbornness in her mother, who stood up to everything: the day, the night, the *chrétiens-vivants*, and the animals. The land could burst into the flames, the waters could dry up, she wouldn't relent. She kept going. She went as far as she could. Every market day, she took a little bit more space. After three months she spread out her goods in peace in one of the most coveted corners of the Baudelet market.

But Ermancia didn't stop at the market. She managed to win over Madame Frétillon, too, by offering her the most beautiful eggplants, yams, beans, not to mention her tobacco leaves as long as a man's arm. Very quickly, she became the main supplier for Madame Frétillon, who even went as far as saving her a cup of coffee on market days.

Lucien, one of Albert Frétillon's sons, unlike his sister Eglantine, who remained in France, or his brother, François, who lived in Port-au-Prince, loved the greed of this trading post in the province where his family had made its fortune. He had married Fatme Békri, a Syro-Lebanese woman. It was a break from convention in those times, for a bourgeois, even in the provinces, to marry a Syro-Lebanese. But Lucien knew that she would have no match in turning goods into cash. He had Fatme Békri Frétillon stand below a caricature of a thin man in rags facing a pot-bellied man in rich clothes. Under the first image, it read: *I sold on credit*, and under the second: *I sold for cash.* At every demand for a rebate or credit, Madame Frétillon, the sweet hypocrite, pointed to the caricature and translated it, with big gestures for the peasants, into a sweet Creole tinted with Arabic: "*Ti chérrrie, mafifrouz,* I cannot, *mwen pa kapab.*"

Olmène, standing behind her mother, enjoyed, as her grandfather Bonal Lafleur had some forty years earlier, watching the men sitting on the Frétillons' porch. Always the same: the director of the high school, jet-black; the chief of police, a mulatto from Jacmel; the town judge, a quadroon from Jérémie. She watched everything, listened to everything, and remembered the rare occasions when she had seen Tertulion Mésidor meet with these men to discuss questions that were beyond her comprehension. Just as they had been beyond the comprehension of her grandfather Bonal Lafleur. It was 1960 and Olmène knew almost nothing, no more than we did, that they were talking about a powerful man, a doctor from the countryside who spoke, head down, with the nasally voice of a zombi and wore a black hat and thick glasses. Because he had taken care of peasants in the countryside and treated the yaws, some men, like the director of the high-school, believed in his humility, in his charity, in his infinite compassion. Others, like the police chief and the judge, feeling that their old-world, light-skin caste was under threat, were suspicious of this black peasant who said nothing worthwhile. No, really, nothing worthwhile!

"*Bakoulou*, charlatan," they repeated as often as they could. Tertulien, he kicked himself for having been convinced by the judge and the police chief to back the rival of the man in the black hat and thick glasses. Others, just how many we'll never know, were right to believe that it would be difficult from there on out on this island to stand tall as decent men and women.

Like all of us, Olmène often wondered if God, the Grand Maître, in his great wisdom, had created them, she and hers, with the same clay as the rest. And if he had put as much care into his creation of hers as of theirs. Equally into those who loved the man in the black hat and thick glasses as those who didn't. She looked at her naked feet, the august assembly of these men, then at Madame Frétillon's light skin and her husband's new car. It seemed to her that he hadn't. To us, too.

Olmène thought of it again in the first shadows of the sunset, after washing her face several times, letting the droplets make her skin glisten like mother of pearl. And again just after scrubbing herself, scrubbing her feet of any trace of mud. She thought of it again at night fall, on the veranda next to the market, when the women, face and feet clean, met around the *lampes bobèches*★ and Man Nosélia's only stove to sip some tisanes and to talk. To talk as though wresting from the night these words that belonged to it alone. Words that they drew from the light of the day, as though a little darkness was needed to seize them. Olmène loved these voices that seemed to come out of a single great body of shadow. From a sole mouth. The flames danced over these burning, bare words of the night. Olmène could distinguish a profile eaten away by the darkness whenever one of the women bent over to rekindle the fire or pour more of the cinnamon or anise or ginger tisane in her enameled mug. Or when one of their faces rose out of the plumes, nearly blue, from the smoke of a pipe.

They took turns without tiring, stringing together one story after the other. Those of tax collectors and soldiers, always ready to extort them for something. The escapades of concubines, the impertinence of *matelotes*,★ the troubles of children. Those of the *jardins*, where they would wear themselves out growing vegetables, millet, and corn. The stories of the most precious garden, that they, the women, kept, coiled up between their hips, that belonged only to them. And the men who had stopped there to rekindle their embers and light their fires. Words of women who spoke by the grace of God, the force of the Mysteries, the tribulations and the satisfactions of the *chrétiens-vivants*. She could have listened for hours to this speech pulled from the thickness of the days. Because the time spent talking like this isn't time, it's light. The time spent talking like this, it's water washing the soul, the *bon ange*.

Man Nosélia put down her pipe only when she felt the first burning in her mouth and the stinging in her eyes. She laughed one last time before soothing the sores on her tongue, the insides of her cheeks, and her palate with a concoction of lettuce and honey. She did so loudly and then spat out a big stream of saliva, scratched her feet, crotch, and armpits in the manner of a cockroach, and fell asleep, a smile forgotten across her lips.

Ermancia arranged the rags on which slept with her daughter. They went over the sales of the day one last time and reviewed the projects for the future: once fattened, the larger of the two pigs would be sold to allow the purchase of two other younger ones who would be fattened in turn, and the new lands of the State would be opened for cultivation.

"Even if, just between you and me, Olmène, the new cultivation land won't give much, and if I listened to myself, I would go all the way up there. Where, in great mercy, the coffee grows. Where the veins of the earth are very fragile, but where the sun is still generous." And then Ermancia sighed: "But that's how it is."

Olmène listened to her attentively while straining to see in her mother the vendor in the market, the woman she had discovered. Ermancia noticed and, just before closing her eyes, she whispered to Olmène that one shouldn't say everything. Especially not to men. "Even if he offers you a roof and takes care of your children." That silence is the surest friend. The only one who won't betray you. "Never, you hear me," she insisted. Olmène snuggled close to her mother and put her head on her belly. To traverse, with her, these quiet lands that man never penetrated, except with the ignorance of a conquerer. Where, however conquering he may be, he doesn't know how to tread.

Olmène entered into the grand plain of the night swept by the opposing winds, thinking of the meeting at daybreak, of the secret that Ermancia had since seemed to keep, of that conversation at night among the vendors and those last words of her mother. She smiled at the idea of this first secret of women. This first complicity between mother and daughter.

Olmène looked at the stars outside, like nails stuck in the sky. Like us, she knew that God had hammered them there and could take one out whenever it seemed right to send messages to the *hougans*★ or the powerful *mambos*. Or to put them in their open palms.

Other thoughts came to her, clear because they had no noise, no words. Not demanding anything. A sigh that wasn't just fatigue escaped through her lips. A sigh that evoked the memory of a man's gaze. The memory of this man's eyes weighing on her like hands. A diffuse pleasure radiated from a hot and humid place inside of her. She curled up to hold back this strange wave. A sigh escaped her again, that nobody was to hear. No one. Not even Ermancia.

9.

In the early afternoon, with some other women, two from Roseaux, one from Pointe Sable, and two from Ti Pistache, Olmène and Ermancia went back to Anse Bleue. Splitting up, catching up, splitting up from each other again. Like a flock of migratory birds. A moving stain, never the same, on the paths winding under the sky and sun. Olmène felt more than ever that she belonged with these peasant women. Open to all the winds. Women in the same washed-out, patched-up dresses. Women with speech in tatters. A force sleeping in the swaying of their hips, in their voices too. Like under the dirt, a sheet of running water, a source of a fire.

It was hardly three o'clock when, on the road between Roseaux and Ti Pistache, they passed a young priest, already quite beaten up by the sun, big red patches on his skin. He rode a donkey led by Érilien, the sacristan of the chapel in Roseaux, and carried a collection of miscellaneous objects—a pot, two enameled mugs, books, a blanket. Sweat beaded on his forehead, at times nearly forcing him to close his eyes and marking his white cassock with big halos under his armpits, on his back, and above his navel. The priest breathed like a bull. Two bulging eyes protruded from his fat face. Eyes that were strong-willed and naive. Naive to the point of seeing his entrance into the world of Ti Pistache, Baudelet, and Anse Bleue as both certain and necessary, and that this certainty and necessity were irremediable. "That's the new priest," Olmène said to Ermancia. "He is going to the Chapelle Sainte-Antoine-de-Padoue in Roseaux."

The young priest, a chubby but tired thirty-something, took off his hat to greet them as they approached, wiped his face and neck, introduced himself, and announced that he was the new priest in Roseaux. That he would build a beautiful church there. "I expect you to come and hear the word of God." Ermancia smiled and acquiesced with a submissive "Yes, *mon pè.*" Hardly audible. Eyes fixed on the ground. Érilien overrated the piety of the women whom he claimed to have known for a long time. Olmène smiled in turn, examining the man, secretly but with a sharp eye. Their smiles had raised an invisible wall into which Father Bonin—that was his name—collided without even realizing it. A wall that the sacristan had helped them build with his words. Ermancia and Olmène, standing behind this wall, glanced over it for a moment as the Father walked toward Roseaux. Érilien, not wanting to arouse any suspicion from the newcomer, didn't exchange a single look with the two women and turned away without turning back, his hand firmly squeezing the donkey's reins. Father Bonin went on, exhausted by the journey but his heart at work, his soul lighter, persuaded that he had brought two new sheep into his flock on its way to salvation.

Between Roseaux and the Peletier Morne, Olmène, Ermancia, and the other women walked along the Mayonne River, bordered by *malangas* with large violet leaves and watercresses like fuzzy manes, with the same fear in their heart of seeing *Simbi*★ come out from between two rocks and lead them to a secret place from which they wouldn't return unscathed, like Madame Rodrigue's daughter, from Pointe Sable, who had disappeared one afternoon and whom they hadn't found find until three days later, wandering ten kilometers away, haggard, half naked and mute. Abandoned by her *bon ange* in the middle of the winds. And, because the surface of the waters could be an unpredictable mirror, merciless at times, Ermancia turned around to make sure that Olmène followed her and didn't lean over the river, trying to sneak up on that which could make her disappear.

They went on. Each climb followed a descent that didn't lead to a plain but just to a strip of land that lead to a new climb on a narrow path bordering a dangerous abyss. Sensing that they were approaching Anse Bleue, they sped up in silence and climbed the last hill.

Olmène and Ermancia finally saw Anse Bleue. Behind them, the parrots coming from the distant mountains cried, announcing the impending rains. On the horizon, the red globe of the sun set amidst the squalls of seagulls. The wind broke the crests of the waves in sprays of foam that came to die on the sand. Anse Bleue was already sleeping. They descended the hill with a light step, almost running, magnetized by the village. Olmène was eager to see her father Orvil, her two brothers Léosthène and Fénelon, and the entire cohort of aunts, uncles, cousins. Everyone.

The way to Anse Bleue had been long. Very long. It led to our world.

A world without a school, without a judge, without a priest, and without a doctor. Without those men who are said to stand for order, science, justice, and faith.

A world left to ourselves, men and women who knew enough about the human condition to speak alone to the Spirits, Mysteries, and Invisibles.

10.

The daily catch hadn't been as good as the day before, because the nets hadn't held up. Orvil left at the break of dawn with his sons, Léosthène and Fénelon, and they fought for two hours with a bonito that they didn't succeed in catching, leaving a sea of red blood around them. The *bois-fouillé*★ had taken on water and they thought that it would best to return with the few fish that they'd managed to catch earlier. On the way back to Anse Bleue, Léosthène and Fénelon scraped the scales and gutted the fish with their knives, and left them to dry in the salt.

But after this hard catch at dawn, Orvil was exhausted. "To live and to suffer are one and the same thing," he'd always claimed, "with our whole lives to pass through our sufferings, heels fixed into the earth to not waver. And when we want to throw out fierce obscenities and curse the hell out of life, we call the Mysteries and the Invisibles, and we caress it, life, like one calms a rearing horse."

Orvil had hardly passed through the door to his hut when he had to intervene to take care of Yvnel, the son of his younger brother Nélius. He put his blue handkerchief around his neck.

Blue, the color of Agwé, his *mèt tèt*. He wore this whenever when he had to work to heal somebody, help with a difficult birth, or remove a bad spell cast over a *chrétien-vivant*, a house, or a *jardin*. Yvnel trembled from head to toe, overcome by a high fever. Orvil made his way to the back of hut, to the family grove. He gathered roots, bark, and herbs, which he crushed, mixed, kneaded in an enameled bowl while singing in a whisper:

> *Mèt Gran Bwa Îlé*
> *Zanfan yo malad*
> *Bezwen twa fèy sakré*
> *Pou m bouyi te*
> Maître Gran Bwa Îlé
> Your children are sick
> I need sacred leaves, three
> To prepare the tea

Grimacing, the boy swallowed three gulps of a green and viscous liquid. Only Orvil knew the recipe. When he went back to Yvnel's mother, it was to reassure her.

Orvil finally sat down at the entrance to his hut, took his bottle of *trempé* and poured three drops in the dust for the Dead before bringing it to his lips. Once. Twice. Several times. The grave of his father Bonal, just beside the hut, between the stones and the wild grass, rose up behind the plumes of blue smoke from his pipe. He remembered the rider who had visited his mother, Dieula, and the month-long penance. He slid into a sweet sleepiness, *nan dòmi*, waiting for the the Invisibles and the Dead to visit him behind his eyelids.

And Bonal Lafleur soon made a sign above his grave. A sober, pensive, even uneasy Bonal, in his thin blue cotton shirt too big for his slight shoulders. And, behind Bonal, Orvil saw the furtive shadow of Dieunor, his *franginen* forefather. Long, evanescent silhouette, high forehead, emaciated face. But he would have recognized him anywhere, because of the scar on his right cheek. Not a day went by that he didn't think of Dieunor, that he didn't think of the secrets of this *franginen* ancestor, the secrets to which Bonal, his father, had been made the keeper.

When Ermancia and Olmène arrived, Orvil was still sleeping, his head bent slightly forward, his chair propped against the wall at the entrance to the hut. Olmène watched the ample movements of his thorax like those of an animal in repose. His motionless face showed a deep fatigue, which got mixed up with the forgotten smile on his mouth. For a moment, Orvil resisted the hand that shook him gently on the shoulder. Neither Ermancia nor Olmène mentioned the unexpected and untimely appearance of Tertulien Mésidor at the fish stall at the Ti Pistache market.

Orvil stretched out and asked, mechanically, if sales had been good. Ermancia pouted slightly and said the routine "Not bad," while in fact they had sold everything, and for a good price. She handed out a portion, just a portion, of the profits to Orvil, along with the soap, the oil, and the cloth that she had bought from Madame Frétillon. Ermancia promised him that she would make him a new shirt in Roseaux. He nodded.

When she asked him for news of her sons, Orvil told her that Léosthène had just told him again about his desire to leave

Anse Bleue and go to the Dominican Republic or Cuba. Anywhere, just to leave. Like Saint-Ange, the father of Ilménèse's
children. Like Dérisca, that man from Ti Pistache who had left for
the big island and brought back, his words ringing like bells—"car-
amba, porqué no, si señor"— "guayabelles★ like you've never seen
and two gold teeth that speak volumes about what a man can get
over there in Cuba." Philogène, Orvil's brother, before his death,
had been able buy a bread oven for the mother of his children,
who lived between Roseaux and Baudelet. "Just by cutting cane,
Uncle Philogène did it," repeated Léosthène.

"With Fénelon, you can never know," Orvil added. "Never."
As much as Léosthène's heart was on the side of the sun, for all
to see: the joy, pain, torment, or contentment; Fénelon's loved the
shadows and silence. Nobody could say if he wanted to stay or
leave, if he would open his hand to catch a dream or if he hid dark
anger or resignation in his clenched fist. No one.

Léosthène wanted to go to the lands where fortune sometimes
caressed the dreams of men like him. Images were turning inside
his head like a wild *sarabande* and he kept repeating: "*Mwen pralé*,
I will go. *Mwen pralé.*" He had buried his rage to live deep down,
and only wanted to take it out to bite at hope. Orvil hadn't
paid attention to it the first times Léosthène had said said these
words, but he finally accepted that they hurt him like the blows of
a machete. The blood didn't trickle but all the same. So many
people had already left. Too many people. Orvil, every day, told
himself that he would get through this suffering, too.

While the threat of Léosthène's departure hung heavy over the hut, Olmène was still under the spell of her meeting the morning before. Fénelon, the youngest son, didn't say anything, his eyes wandering. It's true that the sea didn't give as much as it used to and the gardens where vegetables grew under the sun strained to produce more. Orvil and Ermancia wanted to settle on the land that the State had abandoned not far from Anse Bleue. The land will keep giving for some time. "And after?" hammered Léosthène. "We will take more. And after?" He said it as if to wake us up, to snap us out of a dream. We pretended to not understand him. Fearing on his part a refusal to inherit, a desire to escape us. To no longer stand on the steps of our kin. He, Léosthène, simply didn't want to wait anymore and had given up on the reasons we'd had for staying and not expecting more. He didn't want to. Wanted nothing else. The impatience tormented him too much. And we could not hold him back.

On that evening in particular Orvil felt that, even if to live and and to suffer were the same thing, there was, in the rough hand of the wind, in the bite of the sun, in the belly of the waters, a storm brewing. It had been too long since he had called the family divinities and he deeply felt the need. He begged their forgiveness for having neglected them all those months. Even if times were difficult. Because the *lwas* are hungry and thirsty, even more so than we are. And it's necessary to nourish them. So that they protect us. So that they watch over everything and close the door to misfortune.

Cilianise and Ilménèse, her mother, had prepared, for the entire *lakou,* some *bananes pougnac,* red beans, and millet, which put a light salve on our hunger. And they assured us that eating together was a pleasant and warming thing. That, in this circle, hunger took its share of us. Orvil later drove away the dark moods by standing up and telling, for the umpteenth time, with grand gestures, the history of Dieunor, the *franginen* grandfather, who disappeared on the other side of the mountains early one afternoon, one February. "When he didn't draw on his pipe, he drank from the mouth of a bottle in which he had macerated spices, barks, and herbs into a *clairin* and only ate *kabich*,★ cassava, sugar cane, and mangos. Nothing else. The Invisibles were with him all the time. All the time. No need for him to call them out loud. They were there. Dieunor reigned over the heart of the *lakou* like a great *danti*. Like a *roi*."★

"Then one day…" Olmène, sitting against her father's chair, clung to it as though to hold back time. And to turn her back on the gloom of age that was already introducing itself. In the freedom of dreams, she returned, for just a few moments, to the circle of children that she had hardly just left, where she found clouds of gold, kings of forests, the insatiable ogres and Theseus, the *poisson amoureux*, as the fable went, the paramour of young girls. Laughter erupted every time that Orvil imitated the powerful voice of his *franginen* forefather. Who loved above all to stand at the top of the towering waterfall overlooking the Peletier Morne. Olmène imagined the *franginen* standing there when Anse Bleue and the world were still just ideas in the womb of Genesis. The words took on a malicious and crazy color, and contentment lit the stars in their eyes and put the first rays of the moon to bed over their roofs.

The mats where Léosthène and Fénelon slept were frayed at the edges and filled with bugs. Despite the prickly straw, they fell asleep quickly. The day had been rough. The pestering whistle of the mosquitos passed over their faces, arms, legs. Everyone's skin was riddled with bites.

Ermancia, Orvil, and their children slept in one—the onlyroom of the hut. In the powerful, reproductive odor of the poor. Orvil and Ermancia's was stubborn, the children's was more acidic, and the adolescents', with their battling hormones, was pungent. It mixed with the stench of rinds and stale leaves, with the pestilence of the hole behind the house that we crouched over, amidst the wild exhalations of the animals—the two pigs, the sow, the two chickens, and the goat.

We were in July, the month when the heat announces the hurricanes. The first drops of rain, slow, thin, spaced out, tolled with regularity, like bare steps, and blended with the rattle of the of rats in the straw. Darkness had fallen and submerged us in its secrets, its strange creatures, its spells. Each in their hut sang, in silence, the prayers to stupefy the *bakas*: ★"*Vade retro Satanas*," and said the simple ones to the cast away the devils.

In the hut there was only one bed, for Orvil and Ermancia. A mattress made of bumps and crevasses that from afar you might think were big rocks. Ermancia received Orvil on this mattress. Without a sound. Without a complaint. Without a word. Until, with a grunt, he turned toward the wall and fell asleep. Olmène kept her eyes wide open, her ears, too. Thinking of certain nights when the stifled groans, the sighs and gasps of Orvil and Ermancia, shaken from head to toe, called to mind a distant tumult of cats.

Olmène twisted and turned on her mat, placed right on the ground, and eventually buried her head in the rags piled into a heap like onto the belly of a stinking beast. Because of what Ermancia and Orvil had just done, the memory of Tertulien troubled Olmène even more. A memory of curiosity, fear, and speculations of all sorts. She squeezed her hands between her thighs in order to contain what was already moving within her. Pain. Calculation. Sweetness. Which, if she had listened, would have taken her back to the market in Ti Pistache. She heard the wood whine under the wind and rain. Like the hut might disintigrate under the cumulative effects of the rain, the salt, the wind. Fatigue carried her into a light sleep, very light. A sleep without dreams. But at least crossed by fleeting images. Images of the *franginen* forefather, of the waterfall, of the magician kings, of the orange tree braving the clouds to climb to heaven, and those of the older man towered above them all. Images she wouldn't remember when she woke up.

For the third time in a fortnight Agwé came to Orvil in his sleep.

The next day, the storm didn't let up. It rained three days in a row, as though it was a wall of water pushed by the mountain that imprisons us. Confinement in a vast liquid country. The shavings of the *bois-pin*★ to cook the food were wet and we had to stay, sleeping late, inside our huts, only getting up to share some pieces of *kasav*, to speak in low voices, to look through the slats in the wood at the cracking of the trees under the rough wind and rain or to listen to the noises of the animals in the enclosure. Then, on the last day, the rain was light and the earth was full of ruts and puddles. There had been three long tedious days of waiting, scolding the children who fought and wouldn't sit still, braiding the hair of girls, of women, unbraiding and braiding again. Telling dreams, deciphering their meaning. Returning to the time from before, the *temps-longtemps*, and reviving rumors. Three long days of words passing through the silences to talk to the gods. Of laughter breaking us in two, tricking our stomachs growling with hunger. Three long days when Léosthène dreamed of leaving, Orvil of a service for Agwé, Fénelon and Ermancia of the monotony of the days. Three long days when Olmène thought of Tertulien, who thought of her.

II.

The opportunities to meet didn't arise as quickly as Tertulien Mésidor and Olmène would have wished. But enough for them to see each other three times in a row at the Ti Pistache market, one time on the road toward Baudelet, and she sang a song that drove him wild. And, each time, insidious thoughts like so many grains of sand embedded themselves in Olmène. Tertulien started to desire Olmène not like she was a forbidden fruit—he was the master and lord of lives and goods for kilometers and kilometers— but like a vandal desires the innocence of a virgin. She didn't have an opinion, except that the time had come for her to be woman. And that this event and this knowledge would come to her from Tertulien Mésidor, a powerful man.

Then, the fourth time they met, unlike before, Tertulien was more voluble and told stories while making big sweeping gestures with his hands. He was surprised by these words coming out of a mouth like his, he who had bitten, spat out curses, and pronounced death sentences. Olmène saw a magician in Tertulien. She said that the Maîtresse, the queen Erzuli Fréda,* had put on her path a man who would build her a solid house and would feed her children. She only had her youth to offer to this man who lived under the same roof as his wife and who had already scattered his seed in the flowers of so many women. Olmène wasn't stupid. But that made Tertulien, in her eyes, all the more powerful.

Despite his impatience, Tertulien waited for the day when Olmène was sent alone to the market. Ermancia was bedridden with a high fever. He followed her along trails through the brush and *bayahondes* that lead toward the hills. He left his horse and took her by the hand. She followed him and, in the middle of the clearing, Tertulien mentioned shoes, three dresses, a house, a canopy bed, a plot of land, and a cow. She said nothing, but they both knew that a deal had been made. She stopped abruptly. On her face you could read neither desire nor hate. Nothing. Even her eyes, which she lowered for a moment, didn't express submission nor fear. Between her teeth she cracked the little ginger candy that until then she had been turning over under her tongue. Leading lightly with her left leg, she traced a half-circle on the grass with her bare foot. Tertulien's eyes shone with desire. He had already made up his mind to possess her. "If she resists, I will take her by force. I will rape her." But Olmène had also understood that she, too, could gain something from this exchange and played this agreed-upon game.

Then, when he played at insisting, she played innocent and raised her eyes again as though to tell Tertulien: "You can have what you want." The leaves of an old *acajou* cast a shadow over them and, despite the strong heat, Tertulien felt something like the caress of a breeze.

Olmène kept her eyes fixed on him for a moment, as if to evaluate what would happen to her that she didn't already know. That she had only guessed by the whispering of the women or by their laughter when they came back alone from the market. Tertulien wanted to feel—the ultimate caprice of man—some resistance, however slight, to have the sensation of taking her by force. Imagining the body under the coarse dress, secured at the waist by a big twisted handkerchief, he already devoured her with his eyes. In her there was neither fear nor desire nor hate, but the expectations of a young sixteen-year-old peasant to whom a man was going to offer a roof that wouldn't leak, children he would take care of, who would eat every day.

Despite his violent desire, Tertulien took care not to tear Olmène's dress. He opened the top and put his desperate mouth on two hardened nipples. Olmène was caught beneath this breathless man who penetrated her without even taking off his pants, he had only undone the zipper. He penetrated her for the first time with a gluttonous and voracious strength, inevitable, and the appetite of an older man to whom such a young girl gave the illusion that death didn't exist. "How you are sweet, Olmène! With your skin like a ripe mango, your *chafoune* like sugar cane," he murmured, drunk on a body that gave off the strong perfumes that he loved so much. Yes, how he loved the peasants! How he loved them!

Several times in row, Olmène held back a cry in her chest, until pleasure swallowed the pain in a deep sigh. Tertulien had the skill of an experienced rascal, but he had to take her fast, very fast, before an indiscrete eye saw him in his pleasure. Tertulien's pleasure was hasty, too hasty for his taste, and made up for Olmène's, which was fresh, voluptuous, and stunned. A light vertigo made him believe for a moment that his *bon ange* had led him to the bed of a river in the arms of Simbi, or right into the mouth of the wind, the mouth of Loko. Far, very far. There where you glimpse death. A sweet death.

On his tongue, Tertulien savored the flavor of the ginger candy that Olmène had just cracked. He was shocked, even shaken up, and swore next time to caress this body offered to him right on the grass. To caress it from calloused heel to charcoal hair and to make it tremble in rippling waves like the sea shakes when it is angry. He promised himself everything his manly vanity could invent on the spot. Olmène, she too, savored a sweetness, just that of slowly melting into her her destiny.

She wiped, with curiosity, this sticky saliva that flowed from her, adjusted her dress, shook off the strands of straw and dry earth that had stuck to her, and left Tertulien without turning around. On the road toward the hut, her skin seemed softer to her, as though she had been coated in castor oil. Her back hurt from supporting the weight of so corpulent a man. The thing between her thighs was all bruised, her breasts imprinted by the mouth of a man. She touched her wrists, which Tertulien had held on the ground. And it was through all these parts of her body in pain that she experienced the first sweetnesses of pleasure.

When Tertulien passed Dorcélien, the local constable, a little later, he zipped himself back up ostentatiously, boasting like a greedy man. And when Olmène passed him still later, it seemed like Dorcélien smiled at her with a satisfied air. His smile was something salacious and *chanson-pointe.*★ Certain that she, Olmène, wouldn't look the same way at the naked men bathing in the Mayonne River. Certain that she would think differently of the whispering and smiles she'd noticed among the women, of Gédé's★ swaying hips. Knowing that she had become a woman.

A lineage will be born from this burning afternoon. From the master whose desire obliged him to fall to his knees and a peasant who opened herself to a man for the first time.

12.

*The stranger raised his hands to his eyes to protect himself from a blinding sun and tried, fumbling in the fog, to search for the horizon. After stumbling backward, he left in a sort of horror, running with difficultly because his shoes sank into the wet sand. He turned around several times in my direction, as though he wanted to convince himself of what he saw.*

*He is now at the height of the first huts of the hamlet, still screaming the same names: Estinvil, Istania, Ménélas. Screaming to rip them from his lungs.*

*Mother, call God, the Virgin, and all the saints. And all the Invisibles. Call them out loud! Ask Ogou*★ *to put his sacred machete on me. Do it, please,* tanpri.

*All that's left for me to do is to not do too much and to preserve all my strength for what is to come…What will come, that I do not know. To play dead. So that they leave me alone. So that they do not come back to me from all directions and spoil me even more.*
*Jimmy arrived from far away. From very far. From the big city. In his clothes out of a magazine, with his two rings on one of which there was a lion's head, and his perfume like we had never smelled…And then the boots like you see in the movies.*

*Now I remember: I gave a shopkeeper at the Baudelet market a few gourdes\* as a deposit for sandals. Strappy. Red. High heels. For the feet of a queen. And I gave myself a pedicure right on the sidewalk. Because, what else to do, peasants, you recognize them by their feet. Even without looking at them closely. Those of my father are flat, solid, toes rigid, twisted, deformed. No nail on either of his pinky toes.*

*The first time, I didn't want it to be with Uncle Yvnel. I hate Uncle Yvnel. Because of what he tried to do. Under the pretext of watching out for us as a responsible adult, Uncle Yvnel had taken on the task of following us in the fields, on the road leading to school. And then, one day when I was going with Cocotte and Yveline on the road from Roseaux, we heard footsteps in the bushes. Heavy and cautious steps. Steps like those of an animal on the lookout in the brush. But, because of his increasingly strained breathing, I came to realize that it seemed to be a man.*

*Before I had the time to think, two hands appeared through the branches. The girls ran away. And suddenly a voice at once authoritative and trembling says my name. I stand before him. He advances, takes me by the arms, I resist. He hits me. I yell so loud that the girls retrace their*

*steps, and Uncle Yvnel calls me all the names: "Jeunesse.\* Ti bouzin."
And I laugh, mouth open, I mock him! I defy him!*

*The first time, I didn't want it to be with Uncle Yvnel, but with a
man who would arrive in a car to take me away from this village of
peasants and take me away. Very far. A man like Jimmy…With his
whole body, beautiful as a distant land, stretched out like a tall flame!*

*But let's return to these men and to these women who won't fail to
surround me. To this hurricane in the night. To my sharp curiosity for
this man like never before.*

*The mist is slow to lift. I am again in the fog of this fable. The cries
of the stranger have moved away but they still disturb me.*

*Something still had to happen in the twilight of the first day of the
hurricane to explain my presence here, a grimace fixed on the cold sand.
Waiting for the arrival of a whole village that will soon ask the same
questions as me.*

*I ache, and I am exhausted.*

*The dawn slowly dissolves the heavy clouds, somber as mourning,
that flooded the sky for almost three days. A very soft light finally veils
the world. Rays of pink mother-of-pearl, almost orange in places, which
graze my lacerated skin, my open wounds, and sink into me to the bone.*

13.

Orvil would not have stood any new trace of Bonal, nor one of
the visits so particular to the *franginen* forefather, let alone a fourth
warning from Agwé. And then he had to chase away all the visions

that assailed him, those dark messengers. No longer any question of postponing it under the pretext that the earth didn't give anymore. That the sea hesitated to feed them, or even that the tax collectors at the Baudelet market or the *choukèt larouzé*★ harassed them. The decision surrounding a service in honor of the gods weighed on Orvil. Especially since he had to take advantage of this time between the two hurricanes. He put himself to work for days. We did, too.

Ermancia soon let go of the pinch in her chest that she felt when Orvil decided to sell the fatter of the two pigs. A week before the appointed date, Orvil left Léosthène and Fénelon to go to sea alone, and, in advance of Olmène, Ermancia, and Cilianise his niece, the daughter of Ilménèse, he took the road to the Baudelet market where he sold the pig and procured white fabric to refashion his *hounsis* robes.★ Orvil invested a lot, a whole lot. Put in almost everything. Like us. And, like us, he did it without remorse. No thought holding him back. No worry about withholding something that had its rightful place with the Invisibles, the Spirits of the family. Despite the image of the rider that didn't let up, Olmène helped Orvil, Ermancia, and Cilianise buy enough to nourish the divinities and honor them all. Those who required wet concoctions—orgeat syrup, rum, broth—also those who had a preference for the dry—corn, cassava flour, bananas and pork *griot*.★ And, of course, Agwé, the guest of honor's, favorite dishes.

We pulled the weeds from all around the *démembré,*★ swept and cleaned the *badji.*★ And Nélius with his saw, his hammer and nails, built Agwé's boat. Orvil hardly spoke that whole week, slept on the ground, ear against the chest of the battered earth as if to listen to the whispering of its heart. He kept himself from touching Ermancia and, three days before the date, began fasting. As though this abstinence and this retreat from the world would open a safer path to the gods, to the Ancestors and the divinities. Before all the grand services to the Ancestors, he thought again of Ilménèse, during the period of persecutions, helping her to bury all the objects of worship, *asson*, Ogou's sacred machete, the *paquets wanga*★, Agwé's blue handkerchief, and the drums. At night, they honored the *lwas*, the Invisibles, and the Mysteries in discrete, secret rituals. Hallucinated dancers risking the edicts of the diocese together to pass to the other side of the world. He thought of the crucifix that he had planted above the only door of his hut. The Breton priests, helped by the chief of police and the judge, distributed them whenever and wherever in all the *lakous*. Orvil had established his grand aura of a *danti* from having passed through these trials without flinching. Without falling, without giving up…

The night of the service, at dusk, the Lafleur descendants who didn't live in the village came down the rocky path that winds from the tops of the hills to Anse Bleue, each carrying an offering. Érilien preceded them. The dark hat of the sacristan contrasted with the white dresses of the women who surrounded him. A hat of black felt that dust and time had discolored concealed half of his face. The drums hadn't yet started to sound, but suddenly the visitors sped up their pace, eager to find us in the *démembré* of the Lafleurs. They came to help us, lighten the load of our debts toward the gods, to ward off their own misfortunes. God being too far away and too busy, it was an affair between the Invisibles and us.

When they arrived, Orvil interrupted the story of an extraordinary cock fight at the *gaguère**\** in Roseaux to greet them. Cilianise took off her shoes and spanked the legs and buttocks of her little boy, who had just knocked over the bucket of water between her legs. Her newborn had finished breastfeeding and rolled his sleeping head on her shoulder. A mango between her teeth, she quickly closed up her blouse and devoured the fruit. Olmène took the opportunity to ask Léosthène whether he really had problems with Dorcélien, the local constable, who had cheated in the *gaguère*. Somebody had reported him. For some months, we had all observed Léosthène stomping around like a young colt. He looked at his father. He signaled for to him to be quiet and held the bottle of *trempé* out to him. Olmène leaned toward Yvnel, whom Orvil had cared for some days before, and touched his hair. A baby bawled in his swaddling clothes and the women passed him from hand to hand. Conversations were born and died amid the clamor of the drummers who beat on the tender skins and pulled on the chords to adjust them to the desired tone. We were all there. All the branches of the great Lafleur tree. And we were happy. Happy to remove ourselves from the hardness of the days, to dance with the gods in the dust and night.

The whiteness of the robes drew out the ebony of our skin, the wise, ancient joy of these faces, like from the depths of the night. And we were already waiting for that darkness from outside, that dark mass of trees leaning against the darkness that would soon join the silences asleep deep within us. And everything would be awakened, our pain, our joys, our hungers, our angers.

At the heart of Anse Bleue, in the bareness of a village, an altar was built.

Above it, a white cloth. Lamps trembled in the four corners of the colonnade, throwing shadows over the small crowd assembled there to ask the gods to cast misfortune far away, to petrify it, and to come closer to them, to inhabit them. The *hounsis* kept coming and going, laden with baskets and bowls of flowers, cakes, candies, bananas, sweet potatoes, oranges, and rice, all sorts of food and bottles of alcohol, anis, *trempé*, and orgeat syrup that they, the women, placed before the central altar next to the wooden box—the barge of Agwé—that Nélius had built.

Orvil finished tracing a *vèvè*★ at the foot of the *poto-mitan*★ and, without making any sign, sat on the chair at the foot of the altar for Agwé. Érilien started the Catholic prayers by pouring holy water, stolen from right under the nose of Father Bonin, into the dust, for the gods. He rang the bell all throughout *priyé deyò*.★

> *The angel of the Lord tells Mary*
> *That she will conceive a Jesus Christ*

After Érilien, we in turn chanted the words Lord, Mary, Holy Spirit, in the *aigus* and the *graves* of our French accents, in the sacred sounds of a Christian litany. Orvil didn't understand all the words, nor did we. But this mattered little to a God so far and inaccessible to *chrétiens-vivants*. After all, He and his saints had made us fail on this earth, and we only wanted that they open the way for us to *Guinée*.★

Olmène didn't let go of her father's gaze, feeling in him the will, that night, to brave the world and, with the help of the gods, to take her destiny into his own hands. Orvil turned around and saw his daughter's eyes fixed on him. He shouted at her with purpose.

A matter of demanding obedience. To establish his authority: "Sing the couplets better. You should know them by now."
Olmène turned her gaze to the other side of the room and went
on, with all of the strength of her lungs.

> *Saint Philomena, virgin martyr*
> *Have mercy on us*

Érilien rang the bell again, as though to call forth the nasaly *aigus*
and the *graves* of our Creole. As other men and women joined in
the song, Orvil's voice slowly transformed. It was getting muffled
at times, as though pulled from the back of the throat by the others.

> Three Our Fathers, three Hail Marys
> I believe in God
> *Napé lapriyè pou Sin yo*
> *Napé lapriyè pou lwa yo*
> We pray for the saints
> We pray for the *lwas*

Orvil had seized the *asson* and shook it, quieting the sacristan's
bell and starting the guttural, nasal sounds of the Creole. He sang,
and so did we, until the voices passed from the shadows into the
light, from the body into the spirit. Until the night herself bent
to give way to the African gods, who soon appeared.

> *Anonsé zanj nan dlo*
> *La dosou miwa, law'é, law'é*

Announce that the angels are under the water
Beneath the mirror, you will see, you will see

Orélien and Fleurinor, Philogène's sons, started to beat the *tambour assòtòr,* * without stopping. The music soon ran under our skin, awakening each tendon, each muscle. The songs, louder and louder, deeper and deeper, begged the Gods. Pardon us. Understand us. Love us. Punish us, too. But at least be there. From the bottle we passed mouth to mouth, there flowed a brownish liquid with the salty effluvia of seaweed, the acrid taste of the earth, the taste of the strength of women, and the sweat of men. It flowed in our veins in trembles, in breaths, in bursts, in brilliant lights. A force rose from the depths of our bodies to let us cross, bare soul and bare feet, the wall of the Mysteries.

When he felt we were ready for the journey, Orvil took an enameled mug and bowed in the four directions that direct the world. To the East, *À Table;* to the West, *D'abord*; to the North, *Olande*; and to the South, *Adonai*. Ermancia, a candle in her right hand and a bottle in her left hand, also bowed four times, on her knees. Then Orvil asked Legba to open all the roads to the Invisibles.

Onè la mézon é
Onè la mézon é
Papa Legba louvri baryè a antré
Honor the house
Honor the house
Papa Legba open the gate and enter

With the arrival of Legba, who straddled Ilménèse, we knew that the shadows had been tamed and that the night had fallen to its knees to welcome us. It seemed to us that, all around the clearing, hundreds of drums echoed. Split the air to open the passage to our *lwas*, our Mysteries, our angels, our saints. Our Invisibles were going to burn down the doors, cut down the walls, open up the windows, and, day and night, enter with all the colors of the rainbow, the moon and the sun, the punishments and the pardons, reason and madness.

All of them, one after the other, answered our call. Loko took Léosthène by surprise and blew through his mouth. Strong. Stronger and stronger. Eyes bulging, rolling from right to left, Léosthène experienced his departure on a sailboat pulled by Loko Dewazé, Agazon Loko, and Boloko. All the Lokos *nègres-vents* straddled him with a brutality to match the violence of the rage that lived within him. To water down the impatience that was coiled in his eyes. While Loko prevailed over the waters, Léosthène wanted to drink the night and soak himself in stars. He noticed the smile of a woman from afar and advanced, magnetized by the firmament, pushed by a powerful breath. Loko possessed her like one possesses a lost soul and straddled her firmly for this ride in the great plains of the sky. The drums and the chants intoxicated him, pushed him each time stronger, further. He saw the wild images of unknown lands. There where the sun sparkled and chose him, Léosthène. There where he could tell life that he loved it.

Orvil staggered as he tried to hold Léosthène in his arms to calm the storm. Ermancia wanted to entrust her serious and taciturn son to the sky. But, that night, Léosthène had the strength of a giant.

He seemed to have the world at his fingertips. Still straddled by the *nègres-vents*, he sat on a straw chair in the middle of the colonnade and demanded to be fed. Fed well. He ate till he was full. We did, too. Then, slowly, Loko let go of Léosthène's gaze and released his blood from the fire that burned him.

Olmène, sleeping nearby, couldn't keep herself from thinking that, in a house in the middle of a vast *habitation* behind the Morne Lavandou, a man was craving her. A man for whom she was wracked with curiosity. Wracked with a desire that sometimes cracked open the earth and pulled out flurries of flames.

Then, after Zaka and Erzuli Dantò★ straddled Érilien and Ermancia, it was Olmène, all of her, who was caught up in the great swell of the spirits who have always spoken of the madness of men and the bite of women. With the half-closed eyes of a courtesan, Erzuli Fréda Dahomey murmured, through the mouth of Olmène, words so sweet they smelled like basil, syllables *ralé min nin vini,*★ vowels dowsed with perfumed water. Fréda pushed out little half-stifled cries, crafted from beauty, and started to moan out loud, loud like a woman in love. So strongly that she tripped over a large basin of water at the entrance of the colonnade, advancing with her swaying gait, her proud round hips. Erzuli Fréda, the queen, rose undisturbed, her dress sticking to her skin like seaweed. Orvil approached her, hitting the *asson* right before her face. Olmène then saw the colored, sparkling circles coming out one by one from the mouth, eyes, ears of her father. And, behind Orvil's rainbow, stood the the man of the grand *habitation*, the man whom Olmène alone saw…The man of fortune, the man of pleasure, the man of power.

The drums echoed even louder. The minutes stretched out, infinite, but this mattered little because our dreams needed long and patient strides to cross us and inhabit us. The candles and the petroleum lamps cast unreal, biblical shadows. Shadows of the fables of deep forests. Shadows of the fables of great savannas.

When Gédé attacked Nélius, we were only half surprised. Because it's not unusual for Gédé to come out of nowhere. Without an invitation. And, lecherous, extravagant, shameless, to laugh of our misfortunes. As though to remind us that between life and death everything passes fast. Very fast. Pleasures faster than misfortunes, but everything passes. And that we need to take everything, pleasure and dread, suffering and bliss. The joys and the sorrows. All of it. Because life and death hold hands. Because death and pleasure are sisters. And Gédé, that's his way, he laughs at God, at the Grand Maître. And we were to laugh with him.

We handed a cane to Nélius who, transfigured by Gédé, became as old as death, walking with difficulty and jutting over the pointy knees of an old man, but he wriggled his *grouillades*\* suggestively. Dry movements, playful, lascivious, sexual, indicating that Gédé was also in the thick of life. With every blow, the small crowd gathered around them sang out. *É yan é yan.* Gédé matched his movements to the drums that abruptly broke, and broke again, the rhythm. Gédé aksed for *clairin,* seven chili-peppers, three chili-birds soaked in bitter orange juice, and extracted grievance after grievance, evoking penises as hard as elmwood and flaming hot vaginas. Emboldened by our laughs, Gédé unleashed himself and then contained himself. Again and again. Olmène looked at him as never before. Her curiosity for the man of the *habitation* wouldn't stop growing.

And then, all of us, we chased away Gédé with grand gestures. And the trespasser left as he had come, leaving Nélius breathless.

Orvil and the *hounsis* split up the crowd, giving orders, hitting the *asson* as it echoed near our faces. We were no longer men and women, separate and dispersed, but a single body that turned, turned, and turned again. As though the regular and unaltered beating of the of the *tambour assòtòr* had made one single heart of us all, and the other drums had mixed us into one single body. Emotion was at its peak. Orvil traced the circles faster and faster and we followed him, and we wrapped up the world with him. We wrapped up the world with all our interrogations, all our suffering, all our expectations. And then, by way of turning, it seemed to us that our feet no longer touched the earth. That the dust that they had kicked up was a blanket of light. That the gods woke up in this light and we were bathing with them.

> *Agwè e ou siyin lo`d*
> *Jou m angajé*
> *Ma rélé Agwé o*
> Agwé you made an promise
> When I am in danger
> It's you I call

It was Orvil's voice that started a chant. And Agwé, the guest of honor whom we all awaited, soon straddled him. We dressed him in a white shirt and we tied his head with Agwé's blue cloth. Through the mouth of Orvil, Agwé spoke to all of us. Through the mouth of Orvil, Agwé sent messages, consoled some, reprimanded others because of their negligence. Walked with some who hadn't felt his much longed-for goodness. And, against all odds, Orvil, our path to Agwé, cried for a long time. And we let him.

At the end of the night, we put finishing touches on the wooden box behind the colonnade. We had loaded it full of all the provisions for Agwé's journey. Ten men lifted this vessel together, on their shoulders, while four others carried a goat by the hooves. A strange procession took shape, like those on the mysterious routes of *Guinée*, like those on the sandy banks of the Old Testament. The fragile vessel slipped away silently over the water, dancing on the shimmering sparkles under the moon. And then, before our eyes, sank suddenly as though Agwé, taking us by surprise, snatched it with a firm grip *nan zilé anba dlo*, from his island under the waters. Orvil lingered for moment looking at the horizon. On his face, we all saw Agwé's mask. Powerful. Austere. The mask of one who knows a great deal, a lot, about departures… And then the mask slowly cleared at daybreak. Very slowly.

Life robs us of what we give a hundredfold to the gods. Life takes you and holds her hands tight around your neck and, when she thinks of suffocating you, that's when you breath harder and harder. That's when you twist yourself out from under her hold, without her even noticing it, and you stick out your tongue at life. A magnificent little prank. A liberating joy. The joy of a savage child.

We were united more than ever. Against the dangers coming from those stronger than us. Against the threats of all those who were like us, the vanquished, who resembled us like two drops of water do each other, but who were not the children of the *démembré*.

We slipped on the paths, silent like pilgrims still inhabited by the mystery of a wise, joyful, and distant journey. Our dreams had taken us so far away, in a light so ancient that we staggered a little in the pink and bluish shadows of that dawn.

We passed Father Bonin on his morning walk. All night long he had prayed to the sound of our drums, pleading to God that we might renounce Satan, his pomp, his acts. When he passed us, a desire to speak to us about heaven and hell seized him, but Father Bonin didn't dare. No, he didn't dare. The only place to rest our weary bones was called *Guinée* and, after the hard life that we had lead on earth, no divinity would even think of burning our bones anywhere else. Our eyes said all this, and more. So, for a few seconds, Father Bonin had trouble recognizing us, the sheep of his parish. Because of the whole host of divinities unleashed in our veins. Because of our eyes running wild, shining like the *lampes bobèches* in the early morning.

14.

As Olmène grew, the insidious and raging wind of the rumor blew throughout Anse Bleue. It gathered so much speed that it eventually came hissing through the two windows of Orvil and Ermancia's hut, and forced open its only door. And one afternoon when he was leading the animals back into the enclosure, Orvil had to face the facts as he looked at his daughter holding her lower back, grimacing in pain: unless something were to change the course of events, Olmène would soon become a mother.

So it came as no surprise one morning when Tertulien Mésidor visited Orvil. A morning when Olmène and Ermancia had gone to the market in Baudelet. After the customary greeting—"Honor"— and the response—"Respect"—Tertulien took off his hat, held it to his chest, and bowed. Orvil rose with the feigned remove of a hunter on the look-out and and pointed to the chair next to him, the one where Ermancia or Olmène sat when they shelled *pois France*, picked the straw from the rice, or piled up the *kasavs* once they were well-cooked. Then Orvil went toward the calabash tree at the far end of the *lakou*.

Tertulien Mésidor took a long time to find his words, waiting for the best moment to say them without surrendering himself, hands bound and feet tied, to Orvil. He stayed shut within his silence, certain that the first to speak would reveal his weakness. He wasn't going to be the one. Certainly not. The seconds passed, flowed, slow, heavy, dragging on cautiously, until a nervous Tertulien gave up, with a voice that lacked conviction but imitated the confidence of the conquerer: "Orvil, we need to talk." Tertulien never remembered when and how these words had passed his lips. Forcing himself through a gauntlet.

Savoring his first victory without showing any sign of it on his face, Orvil offered Tertulien some coffee, held the bottle of *trempé* to his lips, and proposed that they go under the old *mapou,* ★ pointing his index finger to the sky. The sun was as still as death and was soon going to make all conversation impossible. "Let's go to the shade," said Orvil. A way for him to up the ante. To pass quietly and calmly over the seconds like over a tranquil sea. He had seen some things in this life of his. Oh, what he had seen!

The dry wind of misfortune, the deaths of castaways, an unforgettable harvest of red beans when he was twenty years old, the strong hand of the gods, the decay of the gardens, the sweet hips, so soft, of women. And many, many other things!

Around noon, we, on the *habitation,* saw Orvil and Tertulien out of the corner of our eyes, sitting under the *mapou,* one with a bottle of *trempé* in his hand, the other with a cup of coffee. Both leaning against an old tree, protecting themselves from the sun and taming time. Real words were not exchanged. But those of the secret conversation to which they had the keys and knew the meaning. Another was superimposed on it. So, in order to bury it even deeper and poke big holes in the silence that surrounded them in the shadow of this tree, Orvil and Tertulien spoke of their challenges with livestock, the coffee that never grew back after the last devastating hurricanes, the sickness of the birds, and the earth so emaciated that you could see her bones. As though their problems were of the same sort, as though they were of the same world.

For his part, Tertulien, believed that in the short run everything mattered and in the long run nothing did, and he accumulated goods, goods, and more goods, by means—theft, murders, and lies—that, very quickly, would be forgotten in oblivion. The other, Orvil, was convinced that, despite the power and money of the Mésidors, the Invisibles and the gods kept them—him and those like him, us—out of the grips of Tertulien and his ilk.

Tertulien played with Orvil. He spoke to him like a child. Orvil played the child and feigned submission. Both were conscious of it. Because, despite his jovial laugh that morning, Tertulien wasn't well. Like us, Orvil knew that behind that laugh hid a man who knew how to buy at a low price and sell at a high one and who, for once, was forced to talk to him like a man who had nothing to offer in exchange. At least, not right away. It's not that Orvil was that good. Orvil was just one of us, a *chrétien-vivant* from Anse Bleue, a village lost between stone, sun, sea, and rain, but he held Tertulien, lord of the land, by something that was worth its weight in gold: his sixteen-year-old daughter.

So, despite the worlds that separated them, despite the memories that had filled the first minutes of their meeting, a strange deal was made. Olmène, mistress of the springs and moons, whose smile cut the day in two like a sun, had just returned order to the universe.

Early in the afternoon, Orvil and Tertulien drank from the same bottle of *trempé*. In small sips. Smacking their lips, their eyes half-closed. Each taking his turn to pick up the the bottle from the floor. Passing it now and then.

It was September. Together they watched the day undo itself. Shorter than the day before in this season. Longer than those to come.

15.

No *coumbite*★ was organized to weed the plot of land on the side of the Lavandou Morne to put down the stakes for a solid house. The first for a Lafleur descendant. Tertulien even hired workers from Baudelet, whom Léosthène, Fénelon, and even Nélius helped to build two rooms with a porch out front. Workers, brothers, mother, father, all, were enthralled by Olmène's transformation into someone who was and wasn't one of us. Olmène captivated us and we were proud, certain that she wouldn't forget any of us. No one.

But, more than the house, the quality of the clay-rich soil surrounding it, the three dresses, the cow, and the furniture, it was the pair of shoes from Port-au-Prince that really pleased Olmène. She had mentioned them several times to her aunt Ilménèse and to the other women of the *lakou*. "More beautiful than Madame Yvenot's shoes?" asked Ermancia, doubtful. Shoes had never really impressed her. "Yes," replied Olmène. Ermancia enjoyed watching her daughter swing into another world, while making sure that her gaze still kept her close.

Before wearing her shoes the very first time, Olmène washed her feet insistently. She had taken care, so as not to be ridiculed, not to wear them in Tertulien's presence, continuing to go about her daily tasks in bare feet. Once Tertulien turned around, Olmène stood up carefully and braved some timid steps that put her feet to the test. When she took off her shoes, it was to vigorously rub her toes, one after the other, the sole and instep of her two feet that, until then, had grown without obstacles, at ease. Of their own will. On the end of the third day, she ventured as far as the path that descended toward the road. After narrowly avoiding falling three times, Olmène quickly turned around, went back, shoes in her hands, like someone walking on hot coals. She prepared a basin of water with papaya leaves and soaked her feet for a long time until she dozed off. Despite the pain, she decided that day to wear her shoes whenever she heard Tertulien's gray horse gallop at the end of the path. She no longer wished to be a bare-footed woman and sought to prove it to Tertulien, to Dorcélien with his air of an accomplished leader, to the women of Roseaux and Baudelet, Madame Yvenot and Madame Frétillon. And, by means of her pains, blisters, and scrapes, she eventually got used to these foreign bodies that, by reigning in her sixteen years of freedom, made her a woman with shoes.

On the road to Anse Bleue, she once met Father Bonin accompanied by Érilien, who often acted as his translator. Father Bonin looked at Olmène's feet before reminding her that God didn't approve of sin.

"You are really Olmène, the daughter of Ermancia and Orvil?"

Olmène nodded yes.

"I remind you that woman must not separate what God has bound together. And that the faithful must baptize their children in His church. That a mortal sin is much more serious than a venial sin."

Érilien translated the words that neither he nor Olmène believed. Olmène lowered her eyes and responded with that submissive "yes" that comes so quickly to our mouths when we want to mislead others. She also looked at her feet, then her stomach, and said that, in any case, God, the Grand Maître, was really too busy to dwell on the thick feet of a peasant lost between Ti Pistache, Roseaux, and Baudelet, who carried within her the child of a man whom Erzuli Fréda Dahomey had placed on her path. And that she hadn't strayed from anything. And that God would love her all the same. She left, begging Erzuli not to abandon her: "Erzuli, protect me. I am your child, *pitite ou*. And you know it."

A few weeks later, Olmène ran into Pamphile and Horace, two

of Tertulien's oldest sons. They stared at her for a long time. She already walked with more ease, shoes on her feet. Her gait wasn't why they had stared at her for such a long time. She understood from their look that they knew. Because she, Olmène, knew that Marie-Elda, their mother, pretended to ignore her husband's affairs and escapades. They looked at Olmène intensely, and she bore their look as she had faced that of their father in Ti Pistache. The path was narrow. They stopped to let her pass. Not a word was exchanged. Not one. But they had said it all.

They were sure that Olmène, like their mother, wouldn't have been so taken by Tertulien Mésidor had he not already broken so many other women. If that imposing number had made him seem like a man who was always ready to unbuckle his pants, it had also secured his reign across the hills, valleys, and plains. Olmène was a peasant, Marie-Elda a respectable lady. That didn't stop Olmène from receiving the seed of the respectable lady's fornicating and powerful husband. But at no moment had Olmène dreamed of taking Marie-Elda's place. That would be unthinkable, and the world didn't make room for the unthinkable. All of the women knew that. The others didn't ignore it either. All of them were, in this sense, left to sharing the same man, under whom they had pushed out the same little cry of pleasure that blurred every border between the respectable lady and the peasant women.

Olmène confessed to us that she'd thought of it when looking at Pamphile and Horace. But she knew that she was, for now, the strongest, the newest, and the youngest. And she simply wanted to enjoy this victory before another, younger and newer version of herself inevitably came to replace her.

Without ever talking to each other, Olmène and Tertulien's sons said all these things and much more. Olmène didn't turn around to see them disappear at the end of the path.

16.

Over the months, the charms of a sixteen-year-old girl, in the thickets, bushes, and tall grass, had intensified the fervor of a man who, with fear, was approaching sixty. He sometimes had her with gentleness and firmness. Other times with greed or voracity. It depended. Sometimes without saying a word. Sometimes with insults, not expecting her to feel any pleasure. He had taken her like her father Orvil took her mother Ermancia in the only room of the hut. By surprise, just when she was falling asleep. But, once he'd finally settled her in the house, Tertulien took Olmène like she was his property. All of their couplings unfolded according to an unchangeable order. To keep his member extended for as much time as possible without really thinking of Olmène, Tertulien always ended up exhausting himself and sinking into sleep. If for him long grunts indicated that something had happened, for Olmène they were just interminable minutes, all the same and without tension, without start, without middle, and without end. Without the pleasure of being straddled by her guardian angel, of having her soul burst. Without the weariness of a satiated body, without feeling full. So, in those moments, naturally, Olmène's thoughts floated toward other worries, earthly ones: the vegetables that she would grow with the help of her brothers, the two goats, the pig, and the poultry, in addition to the cow she would keep in a beautiful enclosure behind the house, the bread oven she would build, and then the trade that she, like Madame Yvenot, would develop between Santo Domingo and the villages here. Tertulien stopped from exhaustion and the two of them stayed there, frozen, silent.

Very soon Olmène no longer felt any sexual pleasure, but settled on learning to let her body give in to the sweetness of things and to the besotted, though already tired, breath of an older man. This didn't keep Olmène from preparing him the dishes that he liked: *tchaka*,★ millet, or dried fish. To rub his feet in a tub of water when he asked, and, leaning over his bent head, to pluck out some white hairs when he fell into a light sleep.

Tertulien had robust arms, the chest of a man who always had enough to eat and then some, the gaze and gait of a powerful man. Olmène, the poise, the gaze, and gait of a young woman subservient to a powerful man. Everyone who came across her was convinced of this, without ever imagining that between the four walls of the new house she had turned that certainty into a doubt that secretly ravaged at Tertulien. Leaving him, after every visit, with the dark feeling that his virility had been put into question. And Ermancia was vigilant about making sure that Olmène renewed her offerings to Erzuli so that Tertulien would never know peace of mind. Never.

Little Dieudonné, fruit of her womb, was born five months after Olmène moved into the new house. She gave birth with the help of her mother and Ilménèse, who had taken care to chase away the strayevil spirits that could have wandered around the house or on the roof and devoured the newborn. Olmène put her hands firmly on a chair that Ilménèse, the matron, *fanm saj*, had fastened to the bed, and screamed: "Tertulien, I hate you. Never again will I let you touch me." She cried several times in a row in the middle of the painful contractions that scraped the bottom of her womb like a knife.

When the child appeared between her thighs, she called him Dieudonné. Because she liked the idea that this son be a gift from God, who knows everything, sees everything, hears everything, gives everything. Dieudonné would be a king, a *roi*. Her *roi*. Called to be the shooting star of the *lakou*. "Dieudonné will save us all. He will go to school and will be, why not, a carpenter or a doctor or, who knows, even president. Yes, president, and for us, in Anse Bleue, he will stop misfortune in its tracks."

Ilménèse rubbed her belly with a mix of papaya leaves, avocado, and quenepier. And, for a whole month, Olmène and her newborn didn't leave their house. Olmène regenerated herself, soaked in perfumed baths to to keep her skin tight and smooth, listened again to the wisdom of matchmakers and all the advice of women ready to woo and be wooed. Meanwhile, from his mother's breast and under the caresses of her hands, Dieudonné drew the primal forces from here and beyond, those visible, those invisible, to engage himself in this great task called living, to grow and to yearn, in a place where everything is defiance and victory.

Four months after Dieudonné's birth, Tertulien killed two goats and two pigs for a feast what we still remember today in Anse Bleue. All the branches of the Lafleur family were there.

The women were dressed in *carabella*★ dresses taken out from beneath their beds for special occasions, the men in their long tunics. The children laughed and ran through the forest of adult legs. Ermancia, Ilménèse, Cilianise, and Olmène finished preparing the meal. The smells came to us, gilded, joyous. Orvil sat down for a moment, silent, looking at all those he loved reunited there. All the branches of the great Lafleur tree. In the distance, the sea was beautiful and gentle. A light wind from the mountains shook the trees. Orvil closed his eyes and breathed with contentment. Like one does when holding a rare gift.

This was the one and only time we had leftovers. Irrefutable proof, if there were any, that the feast had been grandiose. That we had it for our *grand goût*. Tertulien Mésidor hadn't skimped on anything: the *tchaka*, the goat boudin, grilled goat, pork *griot*, *lalo*★ rice, chicken in Creole sauce, the *bananes pesées*,★ crab, *djon-djon*★ rice.

We ate like it was our last meal. Like famine was at our heels and threatening to catch us. Right away. Like the food of the world would disappear forever. Like death already held our hand. We ate greedily. To be full. We ate with pleasure, mixed with the panic and dread of losing it forever. Our pleasure grew tenfold. The men undid the first buttons of their tunics and the women loosened their sashes. We ate to be drunk, *désounin*.

With our dresses and our tunics stained with sauce and our hands greasy, all afternoon, we ladies and gentlemen danced the quadrille, the minuet, like the time when our ancestors, behind their huts, imitated the court of the kings of France. Some musicians came at Tertulien's request from the other side of the

Lavandou Morne and had us dance to the sound of the drum, the flute, the tambourine: "*Kwazé les pas.*"

Misfortune was soon going to crack open our lives, but we didn't know that yet. We didn't know that it was the last time the Lafleur descendants would be together. Everyone. We didn't suspect that events, following a wilder and wilder course, would seal and consecrate separations, departures and deaths, from which we'd never return. Never…

We left at dusk, with the sweetness of a satisfaction that knew no bounds. Tertulien Mésidor watched the crowd walk away in its final laughs, some men staggering in the darkness, and the easy-going women with their swaying gait. He turned around and for a long moment admired Olmène's blazing hips, her eyes that had struck him at the Ti Pistache market, the immense silence in which he so loved to forget himself. And Tertulien told himself that he was a powerful man, that he was quite lucky.

17.

In September 1963, misfortune was going to make deep cuts in the lives of thousands of men and women. Furtive silhouettes skimmed the walls during the night in Port-au-Prince to avoid the headlights of the DKWs. With their helmets, their guns, the blue shadows of the militiamen advanced in the DKWs, combing the insides of the city. They marched in the shadows, forming a hateful mob, chasing after the feverish, trembling shadows that slipped between the trees, hurrying themselves through the dark corridors, trying to blend into the doors, the fences, the windows. It was the beat of their own heart and the breath of their own throat that held up these frail silhouettes and made them go forward, blind, panicked. And all this whispering, this breath, these cries, this screeching of tires lifted the cruel spirits of the night. Then, the trembling shadows watched out for the steps on the asphalt, blood fixed with fear in their veins, until they were caught in the headlights of a DKW, like a prelude to their second death, the real one. Until a cry, a long sharp blade, slashed the night.

In September 1963, the man in the black hat and thick glasses covered the city in a big black veil. Port-au-Prince, blind, falling, on her knees, couldn't even see her own misfortune and lowered her head amid the cries of stray dogs.

In Anse Bleue, we only knew afterward. By word of the careful and fearful mouths of those rare travelers who returned from the big city. We couldn't see the shadows coming for us at breakneck speed. We were far. Really too far. Even so, it wasn't going to take long for our life, too, to shrivel, for the ground to crack under our feet, for the light dresses of women to darken to the color of grief. Only later did we see death spread over us like a frightful sun.

At the very start of September 1962, Dorcélien had passed from one village to another to announce that the trucks would be coming to look for men, to bring them to Port-au-Prince. For rallies in honor of the man in the black hat and thick glasses. He repeated it every time with the firm voice of a man in control and the feverish excitement of a *divinòr.*★ The confusion was made greater for us all, and the vertigo of young men like Léosthène deeper.

Dorcélien came to Anse Bleue one afternoon. After the usual greetings, he went to great lengths to praise the the merits of such a trip, which was going to finally cast away misfortune. "Port-au-Prince has that power," thought Léosthène who, intrigued, came closer to Dorcélien. Some images already rose behind his eyelids. Dorcélien, guessing that his prey was ready to take the bait, carried on: "And who knows if, by luck, some will soon wear a blue uni-form? Who knows?" He pronounced these words slowly, weighing the consonants and prolonging the vowels, making his words reso-nate as though they were the matter of a powerful and good *lwa*. A fire burned in Léosthène's eyes that said it all. This life that had dragged its feet all throughout his years had finally come to knock on his door. This door, he would open it very wide and let life take him and carry him away on its wings. Nobody would stop him. Nobody. Orvil's eyes said the opposite, that Port-au-Prince was too far and that you couldn't, without consequences and without regrets, ignore the past. The land. The blood. To make your own rules. Somewhere else. No, you couldn't do that! Dorcélien, feeling that Léosthène was ready enough and on board with his cause, didn't hesitate to spell it out for him: "Léosthène, I'll be waiting for you tomorrow in Baudelet, in front of Frétillon's store." And added, avoiding Orvil's eyes: "I want brave men like you. Real ones. Those who aren't afraid." To drive the point home and forever hollow out the distance between father and son, he concluded: "Men who do not wear their pants just for the beauty of the fabric."

That same afternoon Léosthène went to Olmène's.

"Sister, there's a lot to do in Port-au-Prince."

"Why Port-au-Prince and not Santo Domingo, where you could cut sugar cane, or even Nassau or the Turks and Caicos like Fleurinor, and return with pockets full of money," Olmène retorted, not understanding Léosthène's sudden rush.

Santo Domingo, she'd spoken about it to him so much, and, sometimes, it made her eyes shine. But the wait had gnawed at Léosthène's patience, to the bone. And, just as he hadn't found the words to explain his impatience, the words to announce his departure got all muddled in his mouth. He just wrapped Olmène in his arms and then went on to share his decision with his father.

Léosthène got up in the middle of the night, resolute from that point forward to put an end to his fight with the earth, the waters, and the sun. He embraced Orvil, Ermancia, and Fénelon, and left. Nothing could have come in the way of his persistence. Nothing. Orvil inhaled the fresh air of the night and took time to close the door that his son had opened on the silence and the shadows. In front of Frétillon's store, Léosthène pulled himself onto the back of a truck with other men like livestock. In piles. Squeezed against each other. Back to back. Nose to nose. The only thing missing was the cries of pigs, donkeys, or cows. But nothing could stop Léosthène. Nothing. Not the burning air. Not the odor of the sweat that almost suffocated him. Not the rocks and the dust on which the truck painstakingly advanced. Not the dangerous bridges of the Lavandou Morne. Which at any moment could send them down the precipice of eternity. Which had already sent many *ad patres* there

Anse Bleue, Pointe Sable, Ti Pistache, and the towns, hamlets, and villages all around had been stripped of some of their bravest men. Among those who stayed, some tried desperately but silently to soothe a land that sulked, chasing the memory of the trucks. Those who didn't silence themselves were caught up in blue fever of the militia and spoke out loud. For us, in the *lakou,* there were, like everywhere, the silent ones and those who spoke.

Father Bonin, feeling our wavering, did his best to refresh our understanding of the nature of sins and the difference between them, the venial, like little lies, and the cardinal—except gluttony, which he took off his list because we hardly ate enough to stave off hunger. With the mortal sins, he stressed the horror of *plaçage*: ★ "A man and a woman must be united before God." Then he went from house to house to speak of the blood of Jesus sacrificed on the Cross, the baptism of children of God, and the courage to weather the storm, no matter where it came from, with Christ as an example. He baptized at every turn, forcibly married two or three couples who accepted the *bénir le péché* in his church, and taught some children of Anse Bleue to read in his school, beneath the burning sheet metal roof next to the presbytery.

18.

*Neither the stranger who backed away, nor those whom he will have soon roused, men, women, old and young, can do much more to me. But I still can't stop myself from mistrusting all of these strangers who will surely come out to examine me underneath my clothes.*

*After three whole days of scattering the animals, breaking off the branches of trees, blowing off the roofs, the* nordé★ *lost its strength.*

*I feel the breath of the sea on my back. To the right, a sudden murmur, hardly perceptible, mixes with blurry colors. A noise rustling with odors and the first calls of the* chrétiens-vivants.

*I return from a long night.*

*Because of the water, the salt, and the iodine, my body becomes a sea creature and now, in my lightness, I follow the crest of the waves that elongate before receding far away, very far, to the deepest of the thick waters. And the enormous mass, fermented and brewed, climbing back again toward the mountainous foam to break on the rocks.*

*In the early hours of the morning, some other men, all bundled up in their clothes, come out of their huts despite the wind and the waters, and cry my name at the top of their lungs. Everyone outside. Out of their beds. Cowards in the wild.*

*These are the last voices that I heard before that of the stranger and those of two men out of their little houses the closest to the shore. They very quickly caught up to the stranger on the way. Look how they approach me. After these three days of the hurricane, like Lazarus straight out of the tomb, but without Jesus, like in the bible of Pastor Fortuné, to explain any of it. As lost as we were the first night when the plane flew over Anse Bleue. So much confusion these last weeks. What confusion!*

*I think of Cocotte and Yvelyne. It only took one look at me for nothing to be the same again. Jimmy, let me listen to a new song...*

*On the way, Yvelyne, Cocotte and I met Jimmy, the only foreigner in the five villages and hamlets around here. The only one. He wasn't all that foreign anyway. Arrived a few weeks ago. To take back his rights to the land, and the land itself. The lands of the Mésidors. And I, I followed him. Little animal on the look out in the wild grass. I clung to his heels.*

*From his new, flashy 4x4, the voice of Wyclef Jean at full blast called 911—*"Someone please call 911"—*and Mary J. Blige responded:* "This is the kind of love my mother used to warn me about." *A sound-system to burst your eardrums. And Cocotte, Yvelyne, and I, we couldn't keep still. We approached in lockstep, legs restless, bodies cool. It was nothing like the Invincibles, the orchestra in Roseaux. Shabby. Lousy. Just two guitars, three drums, a keyboard. And that's it. A singer with a reedy voice, a prominent Adam's apple, and short-sightedness like you wouldn't believe. Without any taste of the outside world. Without any taste of the big city. Without any threat and without danger along the great meandering of life.*

*A little longer and we would have danced on the bumpy road just like in the discotheque. Like at the Blue Moon in Baudelet where we, Cocotte, Yvelyne, and I, dreamed of being taken one day. One day…So we just laughed under our breath, quickening our steps. Being the most curious, I was the only to turn around.*

*Jimmy lowered the window and revealed a face that was neither handsome nor inviting. And me, neither beautiful nor inviting, I wanted to turn on a flashlight. To see…Nothing but to see.*

*I called him "Monsieur" and that pleased him, but deep down, I wanted to cry out to him:* "Oh, Jimmy, my love! I make it seem like I don't see you, while for weeks, I only see you."

*We are getting to know Baudelet well. We spend the weekdays with cousins. The big school is a few blocks from Blue Moon. No way for Cocotte, Yvelyne, and I to avoid it. And then, after school, we had agreed to swap our closed-toed schoolgirl shoes for the sandals of flirts. On the morn-ing in question, like always, two of us would agree leave the field open to whomever Jimmy looked at first. I swore it would be me. I had spoken to him in silence so many times. More clearly than if I had cried with all my strength. He wanted to let us stew in our own juices. Me more than the others. In this affair, Jimmy had too advantageous of a role. He knew it. Coming from the city. His only job to scour the countryside, for reasons we didn't know. And, in his hours of idleness, to show off and flex his muscles.*

*So we pass before the Blue Moon, our hearts in our throats. And there, suddenly, he stretches out his leg and we nearly fall flat on our faces, and he laughs. A laugh like a drunk man looking for the way home after a wild night. We walk faster. But me, he catches me by the arm, leans over my ear: "You seek me, you will find me." Jimmy whispered, bending to the point of touching my ear.*

*I don't say anything. I don't utter a single word, but Jimmy reads my thoughts as though he was drinking them from a glass: "Come here my love, come my love. My mouth drools with words for you."*

*Jimmy took me by the arm and led me to the stage at Blue Moon. What to say of the place except that the diffuse light reminded me of the moon. A moon in the broad daylight, I told myself.*

*Jimmy took me under the influence of alcohol. On the ground. On the bare ground. He undid his zipper that opened upon an already erect and menacing member. He took off his pants, twisting to get out of them. And without the least consideration, making fun of hurting me, he opened my legs and penetrated me with an atrocious tear. I really thought that my vagina was going to explode. When I pushed out my first cry beneath him, he just said in words that I wanted to be reassuring but weren't: "You will end up loving this."*

*Cocotte and Yvelyne waited for me for a half an hour, not far from Blue Moon. Yvelyne was right to remind me that I looked into men's eyes too much. And that made peculiar thoughts hatch inside of them. Cocotte, she told me later that it was because of the color of my sandals. Red. That it wasn't a color that you wore to work nor in the middle of the day. I told her that it was the exact color of my mood: red passion, red hibiscus. Both of them told me that I would regret it. Immediately I thought that they were jealous. And I kept quiet, like a queen.*

*would like to return to this body from before, my prison populated by songs, by hunger, by the sun of Anse Bleue, by my childhood that still sleeps there.*

*Mother, mother, where are you ? Altagrâce…Aunt Cilianise.*

19.

Normil Exilien, to whom Tertulien sold coffee, precious lumber, and land taken by force from the residents of the five villages over which he reigned, had become a powerful man. Before he became a powerful man, Tertulien had always found a friend in Normil. In any case, when he paid him a visit right after Dorcélien sent the first convoy of men to Port-au-Price, Normil Exilien greeted Tertulien without the warmth and complicity from before. Worse, it seemed to him, all of a sudden, that Normil's tone was one used by a superior to a subordinate. No, he wasn't kidding himself… Tertulien again regretted not showing more deference to the man in the black hat and thick glasses. He had momentarily hesitated between him and his rival, the failed candidate, an agronomist, a bourgeois, and also a mulatto.

"But what took over me, for goodness sake, what got into me?" Tertulien said to himself. It wasn't that he'd had all that much confidence in the other candidate, he'd just put all his eggs in the other basket, and now his lapse in judgement was costing him. The man in the black hat and thick glasses certainly knew it, because everyone knew everything on this island. And Exilien held it against him. Tertulien was certain of that. He strongly resented him for having preferred that mulatto, that beefcake, over him, the little doctor from the countryside who wanted so badly to represent the black people.

Dorcélien showed up while these thoughts were running through Tertulien's mind. While he imagined how to turn things around in his favor. When Normil asked him to wait a moment and received Dorcélien before him, all his fears were confirmed. He felt his pulse quicken. He breathed more heavily than usual. "I put myself in a bad situation." He had to, at all costs, find a way to show his unwavering devotion to the man in the black hat and thick glasses. Find a way, whatever it may be, to pledge allegiance. He sat down and started thinking, the contemplation of the man conscious that on this Haitian land you had to know how to switch sides. Fast. Very fast. In his mind, he went over the maneuvers.

Tertulien waited like that for a good half hour. He had thought of knocking on the door of Normil's office or even going inside. But he had changed his mind. Telling himself that only a power newly acquired by Dorcélien had pushed Normil to give him such a slap in the face. He didn't have a choice. It was this man, Normil Exilien, who had a back channel to the Palais National and not him, Tertulien Mésidor. This man who had caught him unaware and who now whispered things into the ear of the man in the black hat and thick glasses. This man, whom Tertulien willingly called "my friend," until that morning, wasn't one, but rather an accomplice with whom he had already committed some occasional petty crimes in the past and, over time, bigger crimes on a more regular basis. The time came for Normil Exilien to forget Tertulien Mésidor and his memories of their plundering, scams, and crude laughs. He didn't hesitate to seize the opportunity, as Tertulien would have undoubtedly done had he been in his place. Tertulien, who always thought himself to be a powerful man, wasn't one after all. He surprised himself by uttering, under his breath: "The man in the black hat and thick glasses is in the middle of making the land of this island much shakier than it already was. Here where you break everything, bones, teeth, spine, and soul, so long as there's one left."

When Dorcélien left Normil's office, Tertulien didn't quite know how to greet him.

Should there be some deference to Dorcélien or would Tertulien maintain his previous superiority? He chose an in-between, obliging prudence. The man in the black hat and thick glasses had overturned all the hierarchies. Tertulien displayed a real uneasiness. Normil and Dorcélien, they reveled in the idea of this game of musical chairs. And wanted more of it. More.

Two weeks later, Dorcélien went along the road in front of Olmène's house, dragging behind him a peasant, tied up. Feet bare. Face swollen. Fénelon, whom Olmène had asked to come help her replant the *candélabres*★ around the house, stopped dead in his tracks.

Tertulien hurried to take out his gun and to hang it conspicuously over his belt. Olmène picked up Dieudonné and held him close to her. Dorcélien looked at Fénelon, Olmène, and again at Fénelon, then, leaning toward Tertulien, whispered some words accompanied by the nervous and rapid gestures of someone plotting something. Tertulien ordered Olmène to go inside, and Fénelon to go back to Anse Bleue.

Inside the house, Olmène focused her ears on the noise of a pickaxe tilling the soil. It was because the sound of those strikes reached all the way into the depths of her womb, but also because she would have sworn on that which she held most dear that the earth herself was moaning. And she, Olmène, heard her cries. She sang, nearly whispered, a nursery rhyme to her son:

> *Ti zwézo koté ou pralé ?*
> *Mwen pralé kay fiyèt Lalo*
> Little bird, where do you go?
> I'm going to mam'zelle Lalo's

Olmène sang so that she wouldn't have to hear the moans, and to catch a little of the air that suddenly seemed to be thinning between the walls of the house. But questions and suppositions assailed her with no respite. You didn't move around all that dirt merely to plant. Not at all. They had been excavating for too long. No, it wasn't for planting. Maybe they were digging a hole there? Nothing but a hole. But, hearing the volume and the vigor of the strikes of the pickaxe, this had to be a big hole. And to do what? While Dorcélien's aide dug more and more, the thoughts within Olmène's head tangled their threads. So she told herself that, undoubtedly, this hole would be big enough to hold that which she couldn't, didn't even want to give a name. "Lord have mercy, lord have mercy on us all!" Olmène sang over and over.

She sang to no longer hear noise of the pickaxe. Still refusing to make the link between the man she had just seen pass and the hole. When the aide stopped digging, she immediately stopped singing, held her breath, and put her right hand over her mouth in order to not scream and frighten Dieudonné. To not attract anymore of Dorcélien's attention nor to upset Tertulien. She held Dieudonné in her arms even tighter, so that the evil breath that swept over the hill wouldn't touch him.

The peasant was buried somewhere at the bottom of the bridge, in the depth of the ravine, not far from the *arbre véritable.* ★ They must have gagged him so that he didn't cry like an animal being slaughtered. Dorcélien's aide mixed blood with dirt to cover it up. Once their task was complete, Tertulien, Dorcélien, and his aide wiped their hands with plants plucked along the path. Dorcélien and his aide disappeared behind the house, climbing up the other side of the ravine.

Tertulien opened the door a few minutes later and asked Olmène for water to wash his hands. Despite how hard it was to breathe, despite her fear and stupor, Olmène didn't let on that she knew anything. She looked fixedly at the color of the water, hypnotized. She didn't serve Tertulien his cup of coffee. She didn't hear him say that he would return in three days. She didn't see him leave. Her eyes had preceded her conscious decision, were already blind to this man.

Olmène was already far. Very far. Inside of herself and some-where else. For a long time the water would have the bitter taste of blood. The image of the man, his mouth gagged, his hands tied, his eyes big with fear, would long eat away her nights. Ours, too, once Olmène told us the story of that cursed afternoon.

When, three days later, Tertulien returned to visit her, Olmène greeted him with a mix of resignation, fear, and disgust, persuaded that even Tertulien's smell wasn't the same. That he smelled of rot and suffering. Yes, suffering. And, after he turned over onto his stomach, she really thought she had fornicated with the devil himself. At that very instant, Olmène made the decision to leave. It didn't matter where, but to leave. She thought intensely about Léosthène. He felt a little further away every day in our minds and we knew that she would end up leaving us, too. That one day, it would be her body that would abandon us. Just by watching her or walking over to her you could make out the words that she repeated to herself over and over: "I will eventually put one foot in front of the other. I will end up doing it. Saved. I'm going to save myself and I'll be saved."

Tertulien felt his hold over Olmène loosen despite the progress he was making with the men in blue, despite the money he was amassing. He doubted himself, because he wanted everything, the money, the progress, and Olmène. He started to reprimand her for taking too long at the market, for spending too much time with Ermancia and Orvil, and for his meals, bland like his body that didn't respond anymore. So one day he hit her. Then another day. But he came back every time without saying anything, like an animal caught in the act. Clumsy in his movements and words, which he seemed to struggle to find while shouting. Wondering what would help him jump this wall that Olmène had built. Not standing it any longer, one afternoon, he took her by force, holding her wrists to the mattress and asking her with each thrust if it was as good as with the young, inexperienced ones. Olmène, her thighs bloody, didn't respond. Never responded during all the visits that followed. She didn't respond to anybody. Even one morning when Fénelon came to help her with the planting, he asked her, seeing her swollen skin, if she had fallen down. In her mind, she was already on the journey. Léosthène hadn't wanted misfortune to drag him to his knees. Olmène didn't want a man to wear her threadbare.

The day before her departure, she spent the night with Ermancia and Orvil, and asked Fénelon to be on the lookout. Ermancia reminded her of all the lessons of life, men, women, of the earth, of the gods. Orvil walked around the *démembré* with her and Olmène lit a candle under each of the trees where the family gods rested, lingering before the one where her umbilical chord was buried. We followed them in silence, tears in our eyes, anger at the back of our throats. Fénelon, unlike us, didn't cry. He gathered up his own anger to make it into something other than than resignation, submission, or scheming. Something that we all wanted to know but that he hid from us well.

Orvil spent all night preparing protection for his daughter. A little statuette with a piece of broken mirror on its chest that he placed in a bottle of water. A way of alerting the angels under the waters, Damballa,* Aida Wèdo, Agwé, Simbi, and Lasirenn, that if his daughter found herself in a bad stretch, for them to protect her. At dawn, the moment of departure, Orvil implored her to return. Even if it wasn't for a long time. But to return. To not put herself in danger. The Lafleur's struggle had to play out here and nowhere else.

Olmène kissed Dieudonné, who was asleep right next to Ermancia, without waking him. All that Olmène had from there on out was in a bundle of clothes that she hid under some vegetables in a basket. To not arouse any suspicions. To not loosen any tongues.

Leaving the past behind her was an experience that Olmène lived like it was a gift. Like a present. She didn't want to be defeated. She would return from the other side of resignation, of fear, of anger. She would return. But first she had to flee, to tear herself away from a dark future. Olmène was hardly eighteen years old and wanted to summon life. Burn the days. All of Anse Bleue had gathered before Orvil and Ermancia's hut. Olmène detached herself from us and walked to the end of the road with light steps, like she was going to dance.

Four days after Olmène's departure, Tertulien, distressed and filled with rage, showed up at Orvil's hut and gave him the order to return her to reason and to her house, and he even set a deadline: "If in one week..." From Tertulien's voice, you could tell that the man had regained his power. At his father's arrival, Dieudonné ran toward him laughing, on his shaky little legs, and clung to his pant leg. Tertulien deigned to rest his hand on his hair and spoke forcefully to Orvil, who never responded. He left without turning around, amid the cries of his son who called for him. Olmène gone, Dieudonné had become absolutely insignificant. Meaningless. A love child, illegitimate.

After Léosthène's departure, the peasant's death, and Olmène's escape, we were from them on, in Anse Bleue, even more than before, going to be overwhelmed by the events coming from far away. And then we would drag our feet because of the weight of what we ourselves were going to create.

20.

"You are nothing but cowards. A bunch of wimps…You let yourself get beat up without saying anything. Not a single word. They trample you and, instead of defending yourselves and kicking back, you lie down, stretch out your body, your back, your head, so that they can walk all over you. So that they can squash you like earthworms. Yes, that's what you are, earthworms."

Father Bonin had chosen to speak to us about anger that Sunday. His skin had taken on a red that we'd never seen before. Unleashed, he gave his sermon with great vigor. Had he drunk more wine than usual? We didn't know. But his voice was hoarse like that of an old drunkard. In any case, it was through this raspy voice that the word of God passed. And, if you were to believe what Father Bonin said, God didn't love us very much that Sunday.

We told ourselves that maybe a frightening *lwa Pétro*★ danced inside Father Bonin's head. He was really angry at us. At those who left villages and hamlets on the backs of trucks. At those who took them away. At those who picked them up. At us, who let them leave. "And the land, tell me, who is going fight for her?"

Taken by surprise, we did not flinch, some of us were wrapped up in a scapular, some in a rosary, and others in both. Hiding our shock well, we didn't even let the slightest comment pass between us. Not a word. We didn't move. Encased tighter than ever in our Sunday best, our only. In our stoicism. In our peasant silence. Apparently, Father Bonin was aware of events and things that we weren't. The news of those more powerful than us, the news of the *grands Nègres* and the *grands Blancs*. The things we had no control over and wanted to stay away from.

Dorcélien left the church in a fury, shaking his finger at Father Bonin, who stopped for several seconds and looked him straight in the eye. Dorcélien and Father Bonin seemed to have started a conversation over our heads and understood each other. Unlike us, who stood still as statues, silent, squeezed shoulder to shoulder, breathing a little heavier than usual. This scene only made it clearer to us that it really seemed to be a story between people more powerful than us.

After Dorcélien left, Father Bonin went on: "A child of God is also a child who lifts his head and chases the unbelievers like Jesus with the merchants of the Temple. You do not have to accept everything, swallow everything without saying a word, without opposing any resistance. They will annihilate you to the end if you say nothing. If you don't raise a stick to strike the enemy."

We nodded softly. Perhaps without realizing it, because none of us wanted to have anything to do with Dorcélien.

Is it because of this slight movement that Father Bonin could read on our faces that we were relieved by Dorcélien's departure? Hard to tell. He made himself even more conciliatory when he added, in a Creole that he was starting to master:

"Well, I know you. You really think that I don't know that you come to church, that you kneel, that you receive the body of Christ and that, once you return to your homes, you abandon yourselves to the rites of savages! Yes, savages! So I am going to tell you, I am, what will happen to you: the night will no longer give way to day, the plants will soon become stones, that's right. The fish will only be memories in your dry nets. And your animals will no longer reproduce. That will be the will of God. Amen."

And we responded: "Amen."

Then Father Bonin forcefully called Yvnel, who came forward in his all-white clothes of an altar boy. His voice was still as unrecognizable when he tackled the song in Latin. One of the songs whose tones we had come to learn just by listening. So we repeated with him, but louder than usual, so as to relieve a weight in our chest:

> *Agnus Dei*
> *Qui tollis peccata mundi*

The songs rose within us like a sun, giving us a little respite. Some, arms open and extended toward the sky, swayed from right to left. Calling at once God, the saints, and the *lwas* to our rescue.

> *Dona eis requiem sempiternam*

Once the mass was over, Ermancia slipped in among the faithful, still under the effect of Father Bonin's sermon. She had to speak with the Virgin, whose statue crowned the entrance, to the right of the church, just in front of Saint Antoine de Padoue's.

She opened both of her arms and lowered her head to tell her, the Virgin, that she was still waiting for the miracles but didn't see them coming. That her patience was wearing thin. That she had asked her for Olmène and Léosthène to send a sign. At least once. That she would soon turn toward those more powerful than her: Saint Jacques, the archangel Gabriel, or Saint Patrick. Yes, absolutely. Ermancia, disappointed and angry, hit the statue with her palm and railed against the Virgin: "You are there, standing, doing nothing, not lifting a finger for your children. Since the time I asked you to give me news of Olmène and Léosthène. But I got nothing. Absolutely nothing." Ermancia didn't hear Father Bonin approach. When she turned around and saw him, she quickly changed her blows into sweet caresses. Father Bonin watched her from the corner of his eye, dubious, knowing that Ermancia wasn't speaking to the Virgin Mother dying on her knees, but rather to Erzuli Dantò with the scar on her cheek, protecting her child against the winds, hunger, the sun, the evil spirits. Ermancia closed her eyes piously, made the sign of the cross, and left, head down, after greeting father Bonin.

"That's it, Madame Orvil, that's it."

Father Bonin had come to love us just as we were. We had come to love his tough tenderness. Yet he didn't ever really understand us. We never really understood him either. Never. But was that the most important thing? We would never have let anyone touch a hair on his head, and he would have defended us against an entire army.

Father Bonin's sermon didn't stop Fénelon from joining the blue militia two weeks later. Father Bonin could have left and gone home at any moment. Where he wouldn't be afraid. Where nobody would come to seize his lands, steal his animals, or drag his sister away. We had nowhere to go. And, since fear was gaining ground around us, in Anse Blue, Fénelon chose to be on the side of those who doled it out. On the side of those with the black glasses, machetes, red scarfs, and revolvers. Not on the other side, among those who suffered the fear. With no rule of law to block the road to fear, he chose to be the only law, and to generate fear himself.

Fénelon enlisted as soon as somebody proposed it to him, a man who'd bought some fish from him for cheap in Ti Pistache, to sell it at a high price in Baudelet or even as far as Port-au-Prince. The man introduced him to Toufik Békri, Madame Frétillon's brother, who had transformed one of the Békri houses into a headquarters for the men in blue. Toufik Békri was the unit commander.

So, the second time that Tertulien came to Orvil, he was greeted by Fénelon, dressed in his blue uniform and flaunting the red scarf around his neck, the revolver at his waist, and the machete in his hand. Despite his great surprise, Tertulien didn't let anything slip. Nothing. Only speaking to say: "Olmène, did she return?" Without insisting. Upon parting, Fénelon and Tertulien saluted each other like two bulls comparing their horns, scraping the bottoms of their hooves before a fight that wouldn't take place.

After this event, Fénelon sparked fear and terror in the five surrounding villages. In the merchants. In the peasants. In the representatives of order and justice. In everyone. Every time Fénelon passed, someone became poorer, lost something, or suddenly felt smaller. And, in the presence of those who used to disdain him, who used to look at him with their noses in the air, like the judge, the chief of police, or the few bourgeois in Baudelet, his pleasure was tenfold. It intoxicated him to exist just to threaten them and smile. To make them suffer and rejoice. Sometimes alone, sometimes with noisy company, with Toufik, Dorcélien and his aide. For those who, like him, were as poor as Job, he started by exacting small misfortunes. Drop by drop. Waiting to exact greater ones until the occasion presented itself.

21.

Dieudonné grew up between the sea and the hot, rocky earth of Anse Bleue. Learning alongside Orvil and Fénelon to decipher the signs of the sky. To understand the language of the waters, the alphabet of the winds. To read the clouds in the sky, to decipher if they carried rain. To remember that to go out to sea is to know the time of departure, but never that of the return, because only Agwé and God know. To take out the animals from the enclosure and lead them to drink. To bend over and break your back under that sun makes your skin sticky, under the dry skies that, day after day, close the belly of the earth and push stones over her. To caress the belly of this same earth so that she delivers again. Green. Thick. Soft. To ration the millet flour in the big mortar in the middle of the *lakou*, for the only meal of the day. To distinguish the work of women from that of men and to be served by them. Namely to let the women fly like flocks of birds in the early morning, and wait for them in silence in the sweetness of the twilight.

To collapse into sleep with the density of a stone and the lightness of an angel, to await the visitors of dreams.

Dieudonné had formed the belief that he had three fathers and three mothers. A close father, Orvil, another further away, Fénelon, and a father of whom they never spoke. Three mothers: Ermancia, Cilianise, and an absent one, Olmène, who sometimes appeared in his dreams. She came from the sea or from the lands behind the mountains, dressed in white, and descended a ladder to approach him. He stretched out his arms and then she vanished into a great white cloud.

Dieudonné often caught his grandmother Ermancia in the act of throwing one last glance at the horizon before closing the door of the hut at dusk. You'd think that she was waiting for somebody. Like Olmène or Léosthène would return as they had left. Without warning. Without goods to carry. Their only baggage their feet, sturdy enough to walk to the dreams that had called them. She imagined these same feet, strong as she preferred them, returning them to childhood, returning them to the *lakou*.

Dieudonné grew up with our same fears, those of wandering spirits, of curses, of *paquets rangés*★ at the crossroads, and he learned the spells to summon the Invisibles, the verses to petrify the devils and the psalms to ward off all dangers. "The Lord is my shepherd, if he is with me, who will be against me?" And Dieudonné never took his eyes off his grandfather Orvil as he mixed, crushed, kneaded, and blended the strange herbs, the rare spices, and the dark debris, reducing them into a smooth and light ointment or a thick and greasy potion. Nor when he prepared the *bains de chance*★ with flowers, fruits, spices, and perfumes, for promises that lit up the eyes of visitors.

Dieudonné wove bonds from the act sharing of all with all. Always an unequal division, like the rights to the lands, but one that made us remain together like the fingers of one hand. Like us, he shared dreams upon awaking and listened to everyone's interpretation.

As he faced the world, all, fathers, mothers, uncles, and aunts of the *lakou*, taught him to master the art of being invisible. Poor, *maléré*, and above all invisible. Invisible to the dangers lying in wait, to those more powerful and of all those who weren't from the lakou. "Make them believe, Dieudonné, that you do not exist. You have to make yourself smaller than you already are. Invisible like a lamp in the fire of hell."

> *Nou se lafimin o*
> *N ap pasé nan mitan yo n alé*
> We are like smoke
> We pass among them and go

In the indolence of clear days, Dieudonné swam far, very far, with Oxéna, the other cousins, and Osias, a friend from Ti Pistache. They sometimes swam until they were in the open sea. Their only buoy a tree trunk or a big plastic bucket. They only returned when the silhouettes on the beach had become as tiny as flies, reminding them of the boats that had gone out never to be seen again. And then they all swam slowly to the shore, thinking of the spanking that awaited them and the reprimands—"Vagabonds, *sans aveu*"— that would rain down at the same time as the blows *de rigoise*.★ But the sufferings were much more ephemeral than the enchantment of the sea. Dieudonné never regretted loving her so much.

He often fished for tadpoles or eels in the mud and amused himself by watching the pink flamingos in the marshes. He went with the girls and other boys from the village to the brush to help them prepare bird traps for turtledoves and ortolans.

The rest of the time, Dieudonné ran after a big mango or avocado pit, or the rare tin can covered in bits of fabric in the guise of a ball. Then, later, he kicked a real ball, on the field behind the Chapelle Saint-Antoine-de-Padoue that Father Bonin had built, just next to the school that Dieudonné hadn't attended in three years. "A child in school," Ermancia had proclaimed to Father Bonin, "that's two fewer hands in the house and in the the the *jardins*, and two fewer hands for the catch."

As far back as he could remember, Dieudonné had heard those strangers who ventured as far as Roseaux ask to see Fénelon with the same words: "The chief, is he here?" and left him a sack of rice, two chickens, some Guinea fowl, or some vegetables. In his presence, they always said the same, "Yes, *chef mwouin*, yes, my chief," even after having waited two hours under a sun that burned their scalp, a fly on the hungry saliva at the corners of their lips. Dieudonné always connected Fénelon's power to that of the *danti* of a *lakou*, like his grandfather Orvil, or a leader even stronger than all the leaders, the one who wore a black hat and thick glasses.

Thanks to Fénelon's generosity, Ermancia set up her first shop—with a counter that Nelius carved from rough wood—at the entrance of the *lakou*. The the first real structure built in Anse Bleue. She stocked the shop with sugar in little brown bags, sold *tablettes de roroli*,★ ginger candies, *rapadou*,★ cassavas, and, in season, avocados and mangos.

When she received the first bottles of *kola* from Fénelon, she saved a silver can for each vendor.

We ate better than many, and the fear of men and of their curses was kept at a distance. We soothed our fear of the gods with offerings. More numerous. More generous. But we never asked Fénelon questions. Not why? Nor for whom? Nor how? Maybe we didn't want to know. Misfortune is a low wall. We didn't have the strength to hop it. So we bowed down and closed our eyes.

Dieudonné hadn't known Fénelon's true skin, the one that covered him before the blue uniform. He was too young. He didn't know how his eyes used to be, before they were hardened by fear and blood. Plus, Dieudonné drew a certain pride from his uncle's power. Like us, he wanted misfortune to loosen its grip. But, unlike us, Dieudonné didn't have anything to compare it to and had grown up without any confusion. In this unique knowledge which, all considered, was an abyss of ignorance.

22.

When the stranger arrived alone one morning, Dieudonné, sitting next to his grandfather, was barely ten years old. He laughed while listening to Orvil tell him about the time from before, from long ago, and didn't guess by his look that he was thinking of Léosthène and Olmène. For the land and the sea, Orvil relied on his perseverance and on the goodness of the gods. All of that worried him, as did the rising power of his son Fénelon. Orvil and Dieudonné were mending a net and turned around in unison when a strange voice greeted them in a Creole from the city: "Honor." They hadn't heard the steps of this man, who hadn't come from the front of the house, but from the path alongside it. A man showing up like a prowler. Orvil responded: "Respect," as per custom, but didn't ask him if he could make himself useful.

It had been three days since Orvil, and then all of us, had been warned of his presence. We feigned not knowing, not having seem him, but we were nonetheless watching him, eyes wide, noses alert, ears open. We asked ourselves as much as we could about the reasons that could have pushed such a man to find himself here, in such a place. With us. To find himself in this strange spot on a road at the end of the world. Dieudonné looked at the stranger and whispered: "Who is that?" and clung tighter to his grandfather, and we knew just by looking at him, we did, that the loaded dice of chance had already been cast. That we were going to have to chose between the misfortune of this stranger and our own.

It was warm. Very warm. The heavy and sticky heat. Without a single breeze. Not one. We were used to the heat, sometimes it even washed out the colors. The stranger asked for water and, despite the hunger that made his eyes bulge, his cheeks sink, the hunger that howled from the corners of his mouth, he didn't dare ask for food—the restraint of a man who had always had enough to eat. He was content to look at Orvil and chase the flies who came to land on his dry lips. He wasn't shaven, and the scrapes and cuts on his face, on his arms, revealed, without him realizing this, his clandestine routes, his fears, the maquis. His face, emaciated, unwashed, said what his tongue kept quiet: "I haven't eaten in two or three days. I am afraid." We, we knew that language better than anyone, but those who have never known hunger couldn't know it. We had this lead on the stranger, this foreigner. Who didn't suspect just how foreign he was to us. He suspected it even less since his fear, not being able to keep up with him, had let go for a moment. Fear gave itself a break.

The time came for Orvil to offer him a piece of *kasav* and half of an avocado. The stranger ate with such an appetite that he slobbered and wiped his lips with his shirt, his right sleeve, then his left sleeve. A shirt that wasn't clean. Not for a man like him. His shoes neither. Holes in places, which exposed the grimy nails on his black feet. Shoes in too bad a shape for a man who obviously had to wear clean ones, new ones, since his first days, since his first steps. He had without a doubt walked a long time in fear, fear in his guts, at his heels, the sweat of fear. God, how afraid he was! And he needed to be comforted in this village lost in the middle of nowhere. He didn't ask to hold our hands nor feel the heat of our arms. All he asked of us strangers was that we simply be there for him. To look at him eat and then drink, and then eat again. To remind him that he still belonged to the race of *chrétiens-vivants*. He needed to lower his guard for a moment. Not to have to suspect every gesture, every look, every smile. He needed this break to forget the cries of the comrade captured a few meters away from him. Before his eyes. Some weeks ago. He hadn't been able to do anything. So yes, he needed this presence to quiet his own fear. God, how afraid he was!

Watching him out of the corner of our eyes while going about our own business, we all asked ourselves the same question.

And Orvil, more than all of us, asked it: what is Fénelon going to do with this cumbersome presence? Yvnel, always wanting to play the most malignant among us, even went as far as saying to Nelius, his father, "Good thing for him that Fénelon isn't here." And stopped short when Ilménèse brought a disapproving finger to her mouth. Because the stranger's fear wouldn't trouble Fénelon. It would even give him strength. Would give him the urge to play with his prey, like a wild animal, before devouring him. This fear would fuel the vanity of a subordinate looking for a promotion.

Orvil held out a little water in a gourd to the stranger and gave him some *kasavs* that he rushed to put in an old satchel hanging on his shoulder. Not a single question was asked of him. Not one. By looking at him, we all understood that he held, shut inside of him, something he couldn't tell us. Maybe he himself thought he knew it, but in reality it escaped him. Orvil pointed him to the path the least frequented by Dorcélien, Tertulien, Fénelon, and all the others. He advised him to be careful, to not follow the road to Ti Pistache, and to ideally walk at night: "You never know." The stranger thanked him again. He wanted to say something but held it back. Unlike us, he didn't know how to play with fear. It was all new for him. The stranger was a novice to fear. We all watched him leave in knowing that, before long, he would be dead.

Two days later, Fénelon called us all around Orvil and Ermancia's house to announce that a stranger, a *kamoken,* ★ had been killed, and that his decapitated head had been sent in a jute sack to Port-au-Prince, to the man in a black hat and thick glasses. Under Toufik Békri's order, Fénelon, Dorcélien, his aide, and two other men had surrounded the stranger, then made him get on hands and knees. One of them had yanked back his head, dug a knee into his lower back, while the aide pulled his arms in front. Another had then seized the machete and, in one stroke, separated the stranger's head from his body. The peasant who had accompanied the stranger to the end of the road where he had been captured met the same fate. He who had only showed him the way. He whom chance had placed there on that day, in that place, at that hour. We listened, dumbfounded, afraid, silent. And since we didn't say anything, Fénelon thought that we approved of it. That we gave him the right. We couldn't approve of something that we didn't understand, but we didn't tell him this. And then, there was this stranger, coming from who knows where to seek death in our *bayahondes*. We didn't understand this either. But while Fénelon told the story of the death of this prisoner and the peasant, Ermancia, Cilianise, and all the women of Anse Bleue, without exchanging a word, thought of their mothers, who hadn't even been able to kneel down to listen to life escape the throats of their sons in their final breaths. Like water from too narrow a bottleneck. These mothers hadn't been able to hold them until their hands were red with the blood of their hearts.

Yvnel thought it best to break the silence by congratulating Fénelon for his courage as a true leader:

"You are truly strong, Fénelon!"

The latter didn't fail to puff up his chest a little and make the revolver at his hip even more obvious. He took his machete, flicked it around with his wrist, and responded with the confidence of one assured of his own importance:

"Well you're either a leader, or you're not."

Our chatter increased. When you start out with cowardice, you don't know where you'll stop.

We didn't dare look at Orvil, who didn't flinch, didn't say a single word. Fénelon, perhaps to coax him, held out, like a spoil of war, a letter folded into four, found in one of the pockets of the stranger's satchel. Orvil seized it brusquely, because he wanted to keep this stranger's final memory from being tarnished. Then, standing before Fénelon, he asked him to leave Anse Bleue, to go move into Olmène's house. Against his own wishes, Fénelon didn't dare oppose his father.

Ermancia, Ilménèse, and the others were wracked by convulsions and pushed out a single great cry. The cry of an animal being slaughtered. They repeated unflaggingly: "*Manman pitit*, the pain of a mother is immeasurable." Cilianise held her last-born in her arms and moved her torso back and forth, wailing. She understood how this child would now be her sweetness, her fatigue, and her despair. Looking at her son Fénelon, Ermancia felt in the air a storm that was advancing and would burn her. When he left, she screamed. For him, for mothers, for her.

At Olmène's, Fénelon opened a *gaguère* that everyone frequented out of fear of reprisals, and where Fénelon alone was allowed to speak his mind. He bought *points* and *lwas* that weren't those of the *lakou* of the Lafleurs, and forged a reputation as a healer. He had a sign made that read: *Fénelon Dorival, healer of maladies natural and supernatural.*

In a dream one night, Ermancia saw Fénelon struggling in the middle of an immense field of flames. And none of us, no matter what we did, could save him.

Orvil wondered, after the death of the peasant and the stranger, after the metamorphoses of Fénelon, whether he would have the strength to fight the fight that was coming. "I'm not sure," he repeated to himself. "Not sure." He thought of Léosthène, of Olmène, and told Ermancia that he felt tired much more often than before.

Orvil was the *danti* of the *habitation*, the patriarch, the spiritual master of the place. His uneasiness and his confusion were ours. And he became even more powerless against the dirt and the rocks that blocked the paths on the slopes as we tried to clear them. Against the growing power of the hurricanes. Against the droughts, each more devastating than the one it followed. Against the breakdown of our *jardins* as they abandoned us. Against the big sawmill of Toufik Békri, who rushed to cut down the trees and destroy natural borders. Against the selling of our lands, which were shrinking to the point of making us *chers maîtres* and *chères maîtresses*\* of sorrow.

23.

*The sea shines. Each wave like so many small mirrors shaking softly under the moon. My father warned us. He took the night very seriously. Mother, too. But Abner reassured them.*

*The first time that I brave the night, it's with my brother Abner. Beneath a full moon. We go to the side of the Peletier Morne. An uprooted and deforested part. The moon, high, shines all the way to the bottom of the ravine. Riddled with white spots, it was like somebody had* scattered limestone pebbles. Abner already knew things that made him no longer fear the night. And I'd wanted to know them, too.

The fascination with the moon, my love, nothing but that. I like you. I don't know a single other face to compare with yours.

I breathe the air of the night, in distinct layers because of the moon. I taste the night on my face. Certain words should never come out of my night. The night deep inside. Known to me alone.

I had to force this man to notice me, to force the door to his flesh. Red sandals. The girls are right. You don't wear such sandals in plain day, but, me, I do, despite the looks I got. I do it because of Jimmy.

Something must have happened to me. I was waiting for something to happen one day that would cure me of my desire to leave Anse Bleue. I wanted it, but not in this way. No, not like this.

Hardly any words exchanged, a finger pointed in my direction, and here they are screaming as they approach me. The stranger brought a squat man with him, wrapped up in a garnet red cardigan, torn at both elbows. A third man follows them. He had to get them out of bed. Each of them already is going, I'm sure, out of his knowledge, his wisdom, and his explanations.

Once they'd gotten up close to me, the man in the red cardigan took out a chubby hand to touch me. To see me lying with this frozen expression in the sand wasn't enough for him. He had to touch me. The other, a real giant, seems to have chosen to attend the event like a show, securing a seat standing just behind the two others. They leaned over to examine me under my clothes. But the stranger, unable to bear it any longer, turned me over with a violent kick in the back. All three of them retreated, and the squat man came toward me again, so close that he could smell me, lowering his head to the right, to the left.

*Then he lifts the only intact arm I have left and lets it fall in the mud and the puddles.*

*Birds fly over the sea, white with foam. I watch it rise in milky sprays. Wild. Each wave watched, surveilled. I look at the sea before the arrival of the pack. My secret will come to shatter, too. To stretch out there on the oyster-colored sand. On my stomach. I feel it. I will be the only one to know it until the end of time...*

*The three strangers keep turning me over, around. One way. Then the other. They want to examine every part of me. All of me. To better convince themselves of that they see.*

*Their little game has been going on for a few minutes. I would have preferred for them to leave me alone for good. Alone with my thoughts that fly toward a piece of land where my childhood is sleeping.*

*I am going to gather my thoughts. All of my thoughts, before the whole village descends on me. The squat one keeps guard while the two others go back to their huts, they want to wake everybody up.*

*I hear some cries in the distance. Sure that this time the whole village is going to gather around me. So long as no wandering dogs come to sniff me, too. Humid muzzle to my skin, my flesh.*

*The crowd grows. I have to be careful not to lose myself in useless contemplation. To gather my last strength. I have to make sure to listen to everything. Watch everything.*

*Abner, my brother, is the strongest of us. The strongest among the men. The first to have rushed into the countryside around Anse Bleue three days ago, as the night fell. The first to have cried my name, his hands cupped around his mouth, until his lungs were torn.*

*It's his voice, the last, that I heard before that of the stranger on the beach, who cried the names of these people whom I didn't know and who come closer. And closer.*

*I'm in pain and I am exhausted. The dawn slowly dissolves the heavy clouds, somber and dark like mourning, which flooded the sky nearly three days ago. A very soft light finally veils the world. Reflections of a pinkish mother-of-pearl, almost orange in places, brush my lacerated skin, my open wounds, and sink into me, to the bone.*

*The whole village will soon surround me. All wrapped up in their rumpled bonnets, their faded cardigans, their clothes layered so as not to get cold, their night clothes and night breathing. A man even arrived wearing only one shoe. Too rushed to come see this apparition from the belly of the sea. Right next to an old woman, head bare in the coolness of the morning. The discussion livens as the crowd grows.*

*When somebody asks if I shouldn't be thrown back into the sea with solid weights attached to my feet, a voice, old and shaky, says "No." And everyone turns in its direction. It has enough authority to be heard. The same authority that made the voice shut down the suggestion that I be burned. Not seen. Not known. "You want to bring even more bad luck? You don't already have enough? You want to lay on more? You band of unbelievers, sans aveu."*

24.

A few weeks after the death of the stranger, Father Bonin closed the doors to his church and left for Port-au-Prince for a whole month. He had to meet the superiors of the episcopate in the capital.

We knew him well enough by then to know that it didn't bother him to punish us by depriving us, for some time, of the church's school, clinic, and comfort. Upon his return, he made us wait two whole weeks despite all of our greetings of "Hello, my father, how are you?" In response to each of us, he uttered a dry and short: "Not bad," and went on his way or about his business. And then, on the eve of the the Feast of the Assumption, to our great surprise, he opened the doors to the church and the presbytery, and announced through Érilien that mass would be sung the next day. Standing at the entrance to the church, he waited until the crowd of faithful was dense enough to tell us in his slightly hoarse voice: "I am not going to punish the innocent children of the five surrounding villages because their parents are forever lost." After this introduction, he looked at us insistently as he went on with his speech, adding: "It is my duty to save them."

Our reconciliation was warm. We offered him a beautiful rooster, watercress, *malangas* for broth, corn, rice, bananas, red beans. Father Bonin celebrated mass as we adored it. Filled with prayers and songs for *Maman Marie*, and a hallucinating sermon about her rise to heaven. To nourish our dreams for a long time and feed our conversations for whole week, the course of which Mary would sometimes be Dantò, sometimes Fréda, other times Lasirenn. He knew it, but had decided to leave us to our playacting, convinced that God would eventually recognize his own. These acts were the sum of all our beliefs. Illegitimate indeed, but they were ours.

One afternoon, Father Bonin came all the way to Anse Bleue to talk to us about all he intended to do to expand the school. Works for which he asked our assistance. He had taken a seat next to Orvil on a straw chair, and asked for a coffee. Orvil promised him that all the brave men of Anse Bleue would help him. It was self-evident. Then, to the astonishment of all, Orvil asked him a favor in return. He had lowered his voice, and Father Bonin hurried to put down his cup to listen to what his old friend wanted to tell him:

"Father Bonin, you are going to do me a favor."

"Orvil, you know that I am here to help the children of God."

"Father Bonin, you remember the young man who died at the entrance of Roseaux?"

Father Bonin looked at Orvil. He didn't want to rekindle his anger toward Anse Bleue by stirring up ashes that were still warm, and just nodded his head. Orvil, feeling that he could go further and trust in Father Bonin, asked him to wait. He went into the house and, coming outside, held out the letter that Fénelon had brought back to Orvil like a spoil of war.

"Father Bonin, you know how to read. Tell us what this man wrote in this letter. *Mwen vlé*, I want to know."

Then Orvil called Ermancia, Yvnel, Cilianise, Ilménèse, and all the others. Everyone sat in a circle around Father Bonin.

He asked for a glass of *trempé,* wiped his face, then feverishly unfolded the slightly creased pages. In the very first seconds of his reading, father Bonin started to tremble. We felt that he was about to cry and that he was struggling with all his might against that urge. He translated the letter for us into Creole as he went on, and read with quivering lips.

*Dear Parents,*

*I do not know if this letter will reach you. I do not know if you will see me again one day. But know that heretofore I haven't betrayed any of my dates with destiny. Not one. The path is narrower every day, but my courage, far from flinching, sharpens. I thank you for having helped me be the man I am today.*

*The country has entered into long season of mourning. For the political catastrophe embodied by the rise of the man in the black hat with thick glasses, combined with the ravages of Flora, a devastating hurricane if there ever was one, which left us bled dry. I didn't stop thinking of my brothers and my sisters that this disaster touched: the peasants and the left-behind of the cities. And, to top it all off, now our vigilance must extend beyond our borders, since the Yankees invaded the Dominican Republic. I deeply admire the courage of the resistance on the other side of the island. And we have to, us too, be ready to face any intrusion on this land that we've inherited from our glorious ancestors. The occupation at the start of the century was already a painful humiliation, too great an affront. And, as our saying goes, "Jodi pa demen," we have to prepare ourself for the worst to pave the way to a brighter light.*

*You will understand better one day. If the reaper gives me some respite, I would tell you myself the stories of my long struggle. Or else, the comrades who survive me will tell you that, until the end, I have tried to be a man.*

*I caused you a lot of unease by my long silence of six months, which added to the confusion of my letter stamped from Brussels, and not from Strasbourg where I'm supposed to be taking classes. But know that the ardor that I always put into my studies, I am using it at every second* with the intimate conviction that that there can be goodness in this world and that some are called to knead the dough that will raise the bread of tomorrow. No one sacrifice is too big for such a dream. This dream, I share it with the other men and other women who fight in the Andes and in all four corners of the world. I will return to my studies with ten times as much faith. I promise you. And you will see me sometime, I hope, around the family table. To talk ideas with you, father, or to listen to mother play the sonata by Ludovic Lamothe that she loves so much, while enjoying her delicious vanilla flan.

I do not run to meet death. Rest assured. I am no glutton for punishment. I'm simply leaving like so many others, like Che, whom you've certainly heard of, in search of a star that is not at odds with reason but is reason itself.

It will certainly surprise you to I tell you that I've passed you, as well as my brothers and sisters, cousins, several times on the streets of Port-au-Prince, but that I couldn't in any way let my love and my affection for you to betray me. That was made possible because you weren't able to recognize me. I let my beard grow and I wear the thick glasses of a myopic. I am still somewhere in this country that I love deeply. But, above all, don't try to know where I hide. That would put you in a situation of extreme danger.

I am not alone. Difficult times have come to me and my comrades but I will never waver.

Lately, I will admit, a vise seems to be tightening. Since two of my comrades were caught in Plaisance, two others on the ruelle Chrétien in Port-au-Prince, others in Martissant, others in Farmathe or Cap-Haïtien. Frantz, stopped in Martissant, was shot dead one night in the courtyard of a prison facing the sea. And, before giving up his soul, he

*seemed to have had time to say "Maman" and to raise his eyes toward*
*the moon that watched over the land he had loved so much.*

*I love you so much, too,*
*Michel*

Father Bonin finished reading and kept his head down for a
long time. And we, we wanted to console Father Bonin. He lifted
up his head after some minutes, and spoke to us of similar things
that had happened to his family thirty years before, recalling how
his father had been killed in the maquis. He hummed the verse
of a song that made his eyes shine again:

> *Take the rifles, the shells, the grenades out of the straw*
> *Oh, killers, with the bullet and the knife, kill quickly*
> *Oh, saboteur, pay attention to your load: dynamite!*
> *It is we who break the bars of the prisons for our brothers*
> *Hate at our heels…*

His song ended in a restrained sob:

> *And the hunger that pushes us, the misery*

Despite Father Bonin's sadness, there before us, it was the stranger himself who'd given us this shock. This incomprehension.
These questions. He spoke of a country that we did not know.
Of people who were far away from us. Of dreams that we had
never tasted. Ermancia and Ilménèse and all the women of the

*lakou* thought of his mother. Our questions passed over the pain, the courage, and the tears, leaving us to face an abyss.

Undoubtedly, this stranger didn't suspect the extent to which he was foreign to us. More foreign than Frétillon, more foreign than Toufik Békri, more foreign than Father Bonin, who had drunk from our enameled mugs, ate on our plates, and did a lot of other things that we would soon discover…

25.

Dieudonné was twelve years old when Orvil decided that he was old enough to accompany him at sea. Far offshore. A place where you have to bring all of your courage, what remains when breath itself, for a few seconds, leaves you. He was going to teach him, his grandson, to hold on by the strength of will. And the strength of the Invisibles—Agwé first, Lasirenn his wife, Damballa, and Aida Wèdo. He never left the mainland without warning them that he was coming. Vulnerable, but tenacious and fearless. The *jardins* didn't give much, nor did the sea. But Orvil loved departing at night on the rickety boat, after having meticulously prepared everything, the harpoon, the bait, and checked the oars, the nets, and the sails. He also liked to remind his grandson: "Luck, you have to wait for it, but first count on yourself." They left the shore together before dawn, on a sea that was still shaking its little mirrors under the effect of the moon. At first they didn't see other sailboats, just masts devoured by the clouds, only to be discovered in their totality when they moved away from the coast and the sun swallowed the clouds. Every boat left to its own luck or loss, that's how it was. After a while, Orvil took in the sea with a look that taught Dieudonné the taste of solitude. In those moments, he observed his grandfather's powerful shoulders, the protruding muscles of his neck, and his burned skin, tanned by the sun. So dark that he was invisible. With this taciturn and stubborn man, he learned to never let go of a bonito, a sardine, a black fish, or a mackerel, even after hours of fierce struggle. Not to be afraid of the open seas as long as you could read the map of the sky in the clouds, wind, and stars. He often heard Orvil, on the way back, recalling the time when the sea was generous: "I caught fish twice as big as you." Dieudonné preferred fishing over work in the *jardins*, which he willingly ceded to Ermancia, Cilianise, and her children, to Nélius and his.

Dieudonné missed school. Especially the days when he saw Osias, his accomplice at sea, go by, with his uniform and his books under his arm. Looking at his friend, it seemed that in his own way Osias wasn't stuck in the harbor, either. That he'd also sailed toward an immense ocean. A horizon as infinite as the one that his grandfather Orvil had opened to him. He promised himself that his children wouldn't renounce the sea, wouldn't renounce the *jardins*, but that they would go to school. He would offer them this journey that he had never made.

And then Dieudonné grew up without us realizing it. Long legs, all muscle. So long that he outgrew all of his clothes. Fénelon had given him two of his old shirts, and Ermancia ordered him two pairs of pants from a tailor in Roseaux. His voice cracked and light tufts of hair covered his armpits and pelvis. When he sweated, he gave off the odor of man, of a wild animal ready to pounce. No longer wanting to hold that tender and soft bird so strongly in his hands, that tender and soft bird in the middle of his boy's belly.

When he was fifteen, the crops burned. The Mayonne River shrunk to a meager stream of water. The entire surrounding countryside was devastated by a sudden drought. Hunger hit the poorest, those who had neither parents nor friends in any of the countries on the other side of the water, nor ones dressed in blue uniforms. So it wasn't any surprise that misfortune led a young niece of Faustin, the father of the children of Cilianise, to end up in the *lakou*.

Louiséna, very small for her sixteen years—she could've been twelve—slipped into Cilianise's luggage when Faustin left Morne Sapotille, a few kilometers northwest of Anse Bleue, to sail for Miami, hidden in the hold of a cargo ship. Louiséna put a small cardboard box in front of Ilménèse's house. Ermancia and all the women of the *lakou* welcomed Louiséna with relief at the idea that the oldest among them would be able to rest their old bones. As for the youngest, they were already delighted to see their load lighten considerably. Between the preparation of dinner, the wash, the ironing, and the insults, Louiséna only stopped to collapse on the rags that served as her bed at the entrance to the hut.

Louiséna had a playful face, uncombed hair, two big eyes always ready to be surprised, which all the misfortune had neither reached or extinguished. One day when the she returned to the Mayonne River to do the washing, Dieudonné followed her. And crouched under a big shrub further away to watch her put the wash at the edge of the water, put the *batouelle*★ by her sides, and coat a rock with soap, and hold it right in her palm. She sat down, and without wasting a moment, she poured herself into the work that distanced her from Anse Bleue and the reprimands of all those women. Dieudonné feverishly glanced at the fault line that he imagined beneath her clothes several times. He rose before her and, by his expression, Louiséna understood. She didn't lower her eyes.

Spurred by that look, Dieudonné asked to see: "Once. Just once your *foufoune.*" The words of cunning and desire came out rough and sweet from Dieudonné's mouth. As sweet and rough as the song that danced in his veins and made him swell. Louisena responded with a gruff smile and called him a virgin, a child, a *timoun*: "I won't let a bed-wetter like you run around in my garden." Dieudonné couldn't stand the provocation, felt emboldened, and dragged her behind the *bayahondes* to the east of the Mayonne River. Louiséna didn't resist at all. It was she who grabbed his neck and pulled him to her. When, surprised and happy, he entered into her warmth, he reveled in her honeypot, but, very quickly, he was caught off guard by a pleasure that swept them away. The very first for Dieudonné.

Dieudonné took a liking to this grown-up game that he played several times soon thereafter, until, one day Cilianise, suspecting the affair, decided that Louiséna had done her time in Anse Bleue and sent her with no explanation back to her hunger and her destitution in the Morne Sapotille.

When Dieudonné was initiated, he had a protective balm made of mixed herbs rubbed into an incision on his left arm. He knew that the Invisibles, the *lwas*, are greater than life, but not different from life. And that it's because they lived out their own dramas they are so close to us. They are thirsty and hungry, even more than we are, and we have to feed them. They are the mirror to the present and the star to guide us toward our future. He went through all the steps the *lavé tèt*, the *kouche*— isolation in one of the rooms of the colonnade—the *kanzo,* * until the taking of the *asson*. And replied with submission and rapture at the first call of Agwé.

Dieudonné heard of those that were absent, his uncle Léosthène, Faustin, Cilianise's husband, and the most absent of the absent, Olmène, his mother. One day, a man returned from Port-au-Prince and told us that he had seen Léosthène on a street corner near the Champ-de-Mars. Another claimed to have spoken to him in the hallway of a house in Bas-Peu-de-Chose, and that he had confided in him his plan to return, rich and generous toward us all. Back then we were still waiting for a sign of Léosthène, but Léosthène didn't return.

For years Olmène didn't give us any sign of life either. Ermancia often called for her only daughter, and Dieudonné tried to make a place for her among the stories of the earth, sea, strange creatures, hurricanes, *jardins,* and hunger. Dieudonné sometimes dreamed of this stranger who had left a big gaping hole between him and eternity. A hole that prevented him from leaning against something tangible, solid. He often dreamed of a *grande dame*, beautiful, dressed in white, who descended from a ladder to come speak to him. And, whenever he tried to touch her, she climbed back up ladder, agile like an angel.

One day, a man from Pointe Sable returned from the Dominican Republic with a package carrying some money for us in an envelope, plus some provisions and a cassette, all from a Madame Alfonso.

If Olmène hadn't put the cassette in the package, none of us would have made the link between Madame Alfonso and her. Ermancia fainted as soon as she heard Olmène's first words on Fénelon's tape-player. Olmène spoke to us in the voice of a stranger. "Mother, Dieudonné, *pitite mwen*." From that day on, Dieudonné was never the same. He waited for Madame Alfonso day after day. We did too, but less than him. Less than Orvil and Ermancia.

26.

In the truck bumping along the lose stones in the truck rented only for him and his bags, Léosthène suddenly felt himself seized by fear. This fear that dug into him on his way to Anse Bleue, it was a fear he knew well, one that turns joy into the smell of acid and overtakes the road home for those who left too long ago. Ermancia, Orvil, Olmène, Fénelon...Would he see them again? Were they still alive? This remorse of having abandoned them had haunted him for fifteen years. Fifteen long years. At the bottom of his bag, he squeezed his fingers around the protective balm that Orvil had made for him, and thought of Ermancia's last words that night: "Come back, my child, do not forget us... *Tanpris*, I beg you."

Noon had struck an hour and a half ago and the earth was burning under the July light. He looked at the plain, then at the sea. It reflected all the light in long beams on the corpse-like earth. He couldn't believe his eyes: all the countryside seemed to have suffered a long and devastating illness. You'd think that a cursed

hand had taken it upon itself to slash everything, pillage everything, sack everything.. "Jesus, Mary, Joseph," he repeated. "Jesus,
Mary, Joseph…"

The truck painfully swallowed the kilometers, rattling on the
sharp rocks. Léosthène had left Port-au-Prince at dawn. When he
reached the Lavandou Morne, Anse Bleue appeared to him in its
entirety. The driver unloaded the truck and ordered two donkeys
for the rest of the trip. They descended the bridge with the perseverance that was demanded of them. They had hardly reached
the limits of Anse Bleue, taking shade under a calabash tree, when
a small crowd gathered around them.

The youngest had never seen Léosthène. Cilianise was the first to
recognize him and summon everybody. She shouted "Léosthène!"
to Ermancia, who rose like a robot and dropped the *pois France*
that she was shelling in the folds of her skirt. Ermancia let out
a long cry from deep within her. She gave birth. She gave birth to
her son Léosthène a second time. And then the cries came from
everywhere. The women raised their skirts and ran to the entrance
of the *lakou*. The men advanced more slowly, dubious smiles on
their lips. Ermancia didn't advance or retreat, she fainted in the
very spot where she had stood up. And we had to rub her with
alcohol to make her regain consciousness.

When Léosthène asked for news of Orvil, he was told that
he was sitting in front of his hut. That he walked with difficulty,
leaning on his cane, dragged his left leg because of the knee that
refused to obey and from time to time gave out, knocking him
down. At Léosthène's approach, Orvil held his hands to his face
like a visor, blinked, and, when he recognized his son, he didn't

move, letting tears run down his cheeks. Léosthène's knelt at his feet and wept heartily. He drew his father close to him and felt, in the shadow of Orvil's skin, the death that was working to make his bones stick out. To devour his flesh. Day after day. One after the other. His father was already light as an angel. Léosthène told himself that one day soon death would bite Orvil for good and would cling to him until it made a pile of dust and bones of him, leaving his soul for *Guinée*. But for now, death seemed to be asleep. He had forgotten him. She had not shown up yet. Orvil was alive. The idea pleased him above all else. The idea of life pleased him above all else. Léosthène burst into laughter.

Everyone, the men, women, and children of the *lakou*, surrounded the hut. The great Lafleur tree spread out its branches, and Léosthène touched them all, feeling even Olmène's absence. Beyond the *candélabres* and fence posts, the children coming home from school, the merchants, all stopped for a moment to look at this man dressed for a wedding or a baptism, with his polished shoes and his brown felt hat. The relatives got bold and started to walk around the suitcases, guessing what was hidden inside.

As a precaution, Léosthène set down his bags and didn't let them out of his sight. When he, regrettably, opened the first box, everyone, uncles, aunts, cousins, cousins, eyes sharp like claws, were ready to take, receive, shoot, push: "Isn't it beautiful, this shirt." "What soap, how good it smells!" "I want this toothpaste." "These pants would fit me perfectly." Léosthène soon realized that he would be overtaken. He left his suitcase and boxes, wrapped in three sheets of butcher paper and string, at Ermancia's, and asked Dieudonné to keep guard over what the tribe seemed to see as spoils of war to be shared.

Fanol and Ézéchiel, Cilianise's sons, were sent to tell Fénelon, who arrived right at nightfall.

In front of Orvil and Ermancia's hut, each came to tell their story of the last fifteen years in just a few minutes. Births, deaths, and departures. The earth emptied of its blood, its flesh, brought to its knees, the stingy sea, the eradication of pigs, the death of craftsmen, the disease of the coffee, palms, and lemon trees, the clothes from elsewhere, the worn-out dressing gowns of the women from Minnesota that warmed the old bones of the countryside, the worn-down cowboy boots from Texas to work in the gardens, like those worn by Yvnel and his young son Oxéna, Fanol, and Ézéchiel, the jeans, the t-shirts, and sneakers from the fifty states of the USA. The bad influence of Port-au-Prince was discussed quietly, the dope, the *paille*,★ which makes the eyes of the town's adolescents bask in false paradise.

Léosthène wanted to meet all those born during his absence, so as to remember how stubborn life was, and he had the feeling that the tree was still generous with its new branches.

When he asked what had become of Father Bonin, he was told of his rushed departure from Anse Bleue for political reasons, and our surprise at discovering a little mulatto bastard in Roseaux with the same pudgy face as Father Bonin. Léosthène laughed, slapping his thighs:

"No! Father Bonin!"

And everyone wanted to tell their version of the story. Finally, Cilianise stood up, demanded silence, and pointed out that the little one was named Peter, but that everyone called him "Venial," like the sin. Léosthène laughed twice as hard. We did, too.

"And why?" he asked.

"Because we do not think that Father Bonin deserves to go to hell for having succumbed to the charms of a negress from Roseaux."

And then until very late, by the light of the *lampes bobèches* and the *bougies baleines,*★ Léosthène let the happy hours of the night pass through him and the evening went on like that, drinking fresh water from pitchers, anise *trempé,* or lemon tea in enameled mugs.

In order to not kill the myth, Léosthène spoke of a Port-au-Prince and Florida taken from dreams and left those of nightmares for later. For when he could speak to Fénelon and Nélius away from all these ears. Alone. Man to man. He spoke of the circumstances of his departure. He had met Roselène, a young woman from Môle who had relatives in Miami. He moved in with her, and she was the one who facilitated his journey to the other shore.

"Miami?" they all said at the same time. "You mean you're coming from Miami?"

Roselène's family had helped him find his first job in the back of a kitchen of a hotel in Tampa. Soon thereafter, his papers were formalized by his boss, who had come to appreciate his work ethic.

"Men like that, you only come across them once in a lifetime. I had that luck. I got really lucky…" he went on, and he gave details about this Miami of our dreams: highways, refrigerators, electricity, buildings much higher than three palm trees stacked one atop the other…"And all the food you could want!"

He stopped for a moment and, looking at all those eyes still hanging on his lips, measured the effect of his words. He decided to finish with a bang:

"And I came back on a plane."

"On a plane!" We were dumbfounded. So it was a satisfied Léosthène who stopped there and pulled out a pack of Marlboro cigarettes from his pocket. He lit one with the awareness that this act had just forged a new distance, and then he told them about everything, the numbered seats, the hostesses—*beautiful women, well made-up*—the spaces always too narrow to store luggage overhead or under the seat, you'd think that those who built these machines have neither relatives nor friends, the forms that you can't fill out because you can neither read nor write, and the passenger next to you, whom you don't want to give your address, your date of birth, or passport number to, fills them out for you.

"You were born lucky," Yvnel murmured, his eyes staring at the first stars in the sky.

When the women returned to their huts under the gentle cover of the night, the men lingered beside Léosthène. And when they were alone, Léosthène told them the other story, the nightmare.

"The trip to Miami was very hard. Very difficult. I paid a smuggler. The captain, this man I'd given two thousand dollars to, said nothing to us when we got on board. He directed us with the flick of a wrist. Like the others, I went down the ladder and dove right into the darkness. When he saw that we understood, he went back and waited for the mechanics who were doing the last checks. The hold of the boat was full of bags of salt and dirty water stagnated at the bottom. Once all the passengers were in, the captain closed the lid, and we found ourselves in deep darkness. Like a tomb, believe me. Then we heard the engine moan and start. And since there were women on board, the captain and two of his assistants relieved themselves throughout the voyage. They twisted only to undo their belts and lower their pants, and grunted as they sank into them. Then they would go up, and the panting and hoarse breathing of the young woman could be heard, as if she had just escaped a burst of machine-gun fire and was trying to catch her breath. After a few days, the hold stank of stagnant seawater, jute, sweat, seed, crotch. We urinated and defecated into the water between the slats. And the unctuous and warm smell of our excrement slowly returned to our nostrils."

Léosthène stopped for a moment, laid his hands flat on his legs: "And then you're afraid of dying in this shroud if the wind rears up and sinks the boat. The waves violently strike the bow and the boat rises almost vertically on the waves, as if it were climbing a mountain, before dipping and rushing at full speed to the bottom of the hole. There where you frankly want to rest your head, like when you were a child on your mother's palms full of stars and sweet dreams, and cry hot tears, but you hold back. Because you're a man. So you call Agwé, Damballa, Ogou. You call them all. And then there comes a time when you reach a place that is beyond fear. Beyond shame. And you say to yourself that if you have gone through this, you can be neither afraid nor ashamed. Never. You are courage, you are perseverance. Once this ordeal is over, you feel a form of power. Because of this knowledge of things that others do not and never will have. Yes, that's right, power."

Léosthène had said these last words as though he wasn't talking to us, as though he wanted to swallow them up immediately and push them into himself.

Léosthène stopped his story because he did not want to bring back too many images, and concluded with a loud, "But at least I did not end up half-naked on a white beach with my photo in the newspaper next to terrified men and women. No way!"

We looked at Léosthène, pensive. Proud, too. Léosthène had prospered elsewhere, by his own hand, without hurting any of us. The tree did not bleed. One branch had grown more than the others. That's all. Léosthène returned, but in his place.

Heavy with fatigue, he wanted to sleep in Orvil and Ermancia's refurbished hut, and not in Olmène's house, as Fénelon had suggested. Léosthène wanted to return to his intact childhood. Fall asleep in a hut surrounded by the rustling of insects like a blanket. Breathe the air of this single room where his innocence was asleep. He slept like a log. The next day when the door creaked and fell open, he looked at the rising foam. Only to break in white sprays. Burst. Then, behind him, the mountain that seemed to want to come closer and devour us.

27.

A few days later, Léosthène went to Baudelet only to find a town in decline. Baudelet was no longer what it had been. The hand of misfortune had seized it, too. But he evaluated how far he, Léosthène Dorival, peasant, son of Orvil Clémestal and Ermancia Dorival, had come when he paid for all his purchases in cash, pushing back a little on principle but not really haggling, his eye fixed on the yellowing caricature that still hung above the counter, right next to a photograph of the man with black hat and thick glasses.

Madame Frétillon greeted him with a broad smile. The news of his return had spread like wildfire the day after his arrival. A Lafleur had taken a plane. Ermancia, proud of her son, had taken it upon herself to share that fact, and Madame Frétillon was the first to hear.

The decline of Baudelet had begun when, on the orders of the man with a black hat and thick glasses, its port was closed. Out of fear of the incessant attacks from all those who hated him for having lost their sons, fathers, wives, friends.

Those who did not move to Port-au-Prince joined uncles and aunts across the world who had already realized that their salvation was no longer on this island.

Thousands of men and women from towns, villages, and localities abandoned the ruined gardens, the skeletons of burnt trees and the rivers that had become bloodless veins, in order to stick together and swell the belly of the city. The competition having dropped its arms and fled the province, the Frétillons rushed to fill this void and in the exodus of the countryside they found customers who made them rich again. With the sales of some *gourdes of mantègue*,* three *gourdes* of soap or sugar, and two reels of fabric, the Frétillons strung together the great semi-legal, illegal, or frankly criminal schemes that allowed them to amass a real fortune. The conversations on the veranda had lost their spark. But it didn't matter to Madame Frétillon, who did not want any stories and liked the man with a black hat and thick glasses. This one or she really didn't care who else, but this one more than the others because she felt that he stuck it to the bourgeois who once looked at her from above, she, the Arab, the immigrant with her bundle on her back. She jubilated twice over in counting every cent in her cash box each night.

Léosthène glanced at the television set just in front of her greedy counter. The very first television in Baudelet. The Frétillons had started a real riot when passersby, mostly peasants just in from the countryside, discovered for the first time, astonished, this luminous square, crackling and spitting out images. After an hour the crowd had grown so large that Madame Frétillon had to call for the help of her commander of a brother, Toufik Békri, who quickly swept away the most docile with blows *de rigoise* and saved the rifle butt for the most recalcitrant, dumbfounded by the images that twitched on the luminous square. And to make things even clearer than they already were, Fatmé Békri Frétillon turned up the volume whenever an orchestra, smiling and in synch, played the blazing songs for the glory of its leader: "Crush them, Duvalier, crush them. *Maché pran yo Divalyé, maché pran yo.*"

Fénelon rushed to introduce Léosthène to Toufik Békri, in the latter's office at the headquarters of the men in blue. A militiaman was sleeping, his hands resting on a rusty rifle that dated from the American occupation forty years earlier. He jumped at the arrival of Fénelon and Léosthène, and hurried to present them to the commander. Toufik Békri, without lifting his head from his newspaper, muttered between his teeth: "Come in, come in." Then, with a brusque gesture, he placed the newspaper on the rickety table which served as his desk, put on his black glasses, and examined Léosthène from head to toe. After a few seconds of inspection, he asked him in the tone of a police interrogator if he was one of those stateless renegades who, once abroad, spoke ill of their country and their president. "Oh no, never, never!" Fénelon cried out. Léosthène did not reply. His silence did not please Toufik, who turned to Fénelon:

"Your brother, the diaspora, forgot to speak Creole or what?" Léosthène cut the conversation short by saying that he was tired and in a hurry. Toufik cast him a furious and murderous glance. All that had accumulated in the course of this brief exchange emanated from it, which had not been said by either one or the other. Toufik resumed reading his newspaper and made a remark that left no doubt about his thoughts: "You're lucky to be Fénelon's brother."

Fénelon was not happy with Léosthène and made that clear to him outside: "Have you lost your mind or what? Or are you crazy? Just go. I'm staying." In response, Léosthène told him that he felt, in the air he breathed in the streets of the town, around the market, that he, Fénelon, and his friends were starting to be despised. There were the germs of unrest, the ferment of turmoil. He had dark premonitions and saw clear threats. Fénelon didn't believe him, and replied that he would be delighted the day he left.

On the way back, Léosthène thought of Bonal his grandfather, of the *franginen* forefather, and of Olmène. He told himself that it really was time for him to leave, but before doing so, he would honor all the spirits and the dead of the *lakou*.

Three days before his departure, Léosthène awoke in the orange and pink flashes of the *devant-jour*. In the azure and raucous noise of the sea in the distance. The mist still lay between the huts. Crouching down, he filled the halves of more than a dozen coconuts with cotton that he soaked in castor oil, and lit them all. The branches of the beautiful Lafleur tree who remained came out. Even Orvil, whose neck was stiff and back siezed-up, and whose legs no longer bent. He, the most beautiful branch still alive, graced the assembly with his presence.

Érilien, old and shriveled, called for the occasion, blessed the offerings. Cilianise, Ermancia, and Léosthène made salutations to the four directions and gently moved their lips, eyes closed, candles in hand, to invoke the protective gods, the Disappeared, and all the Invisibles of the family. It didn't take long for tears to trickle down our cheeks. And Léosthène had trouble articulating the last words. A light fresh breeze worked through all his pores, and his flesh and the earth became one. This wind that tormented the branches told us that they, like us, had resisted everything. Exposed to the dust of the seasons, to the corrosion of salt, to the passing of hurricanes, to the slow fermentation of vegetables, to the fury of men, to torrential rains. They had resisted everything.

Accompanied by Ermancia, Ilménèse, Cilianise, Nélius, and Yvnel, Léosthène, beside his father Orvil, bowed before each of the trees where the spirits of the house slept, placing at their feet half a coconut with its flame dancing on the castor oil. The calabash tree, the orange tree, the mango tree, the elmwood, the sandbox tree, and the almond tree…He saluted them all.

In the evening Léosthène sat down in the hut facing Orvil, Ermancia and Dieudonné at his sides. He opened an envelope and drew out a bundle of bills, which he placed in his mother's palms: "Here, take it. You have to do something else, since the earth does not give as much, nor does the sea. So you are going to build a bread oven. Bread, men eat it every day." This bread oven made us the new gravediggers of the hills and surrounding lands.

On the morning of his departure, Léosthène gathered all the relatives and distributed the contents of his suitcases and boxes. He was stripped of everything. A little more urging and we would have taken the shirt off his back. He left three radios, one for Ermancia and Dieudonné, the second for Cilianise and his children, and the third for Nélius and his. Community radios disseminated all kinds of information on hygiene and health, agriculture and education, and passed messages from town to another, from one village to another, breaking the isolation of the poor who had lived there from the beginning. The transistors were time bombs that distilled the news to those who knew how to understand it. The voices that emanated from the radios of Port-au-Prince spoke about the whole island and of countries on the other side of the waters. And these voices had the accents of impatience, freedom, contained rage, and brewing fire.

Once in the truck that was going to take him back to Port-au-Prince, Léosthène turned around one last time and thought that perhaps, in the future, Ermancia and all the others' days would be spared the exhausting weight of servitude. At least he hoped.

It was a beautiful day. Léosthène, taking in the view of his childhood, turned his back for a moment to the wounds of the earth, to its deep scars, and looked at Anse Bleue bathed in liquid light, the sky and the water spreading as far as the eye could see. Each wave that was sinking, frothing on the sand, would die in a shining net of water. The birds brushed against the crests of the waves, came out of the sea, and took flight over the weary sky.


28.


*The giant seized his cell phone. He repeats every word he hears. The man with the one shoe asks that he not to spread the news. Certainly not.*

At the risk of of attracting a justice of the peace, policemen, and journalists who will not fail to stick their noses in our business: "Who saw her first? Who knows her? Who touched her?" They all speak together. Loud. They do not get along. Do not understand each other anymore. For the small crowd assembled there, the question of my destiny remains untouched until a woman emerges from I don't know where, cries, after two Jesus, Mary, and Josephs, three Lord Have Mercys, "She comes from Anse Bleue. She is the daughter of…"

That stranger, she went to get a sheet. To cover me. As she approached, she did not want to look at me. She just stretched out the sheet to the man with the red cardigan and turned around. The man grabbed the sheet. He is proud to be directing the operations like a leader. He placed the sheet on the sand and asked two other men to help him. It took three of them to lift me and put me on top. We went toward Anse Bleue.

In my wake, I drag about twenty men and women, agitated as though they were going on a crusade like the Charismatics or the Pentecostalists. All that is needed is a pastor or a priest to begin an ecumenical song: "God Almighty, Thou art great!"

Hardly have we left Pointe Sable when in the distance I see Émile, the school's headmaster in his brown shirt with the halos under the armpits that I know so well. He speeds up, driven by curiosity. He stops the procession and everybody starts talking at the same time. Impatient, the headmaster asks to see. Moves forward and looks. His eye almost touches my face. His shock freezes him. He makes the sign of the cross three times then starts yelling, turns back, and runs in the direction of Anse Bleue. I cannot explain anything to him. Nothing. I can't anymore. I don't want to anymore.

I will always remember the first time Headmaster Émile spoke at *great length about the Earth, that it was round. An orange in his hand, he asked me how I saw it. I replied that the orange was round but that, behind the horizon, there was a large hole into which one inevitably fell. He lowered his arms, laughing. Then he asked me to look carefully at the orange and he began to turn it, to tilt it to one side then to the other to explain again the rotation, the revolution, the equinoxes and the solstices. Running back through his laborious explanations. I listened to him, swinging my legs on the wooden bench, elbows on the table, my face resting on my palms, reassured that I had never felt the earth tilt or turn. Imagining Agwé, Labalenn,\* and Lasirenn, still there on their islands under the waters. So, the headmaster, I believed him and I did not believe him. As I did not believe it when he told Cocotte, Yvelyne, and I to come back because the wind would rise and we had to beware of strangers coming from the cities. I did not believe him.*

29.

Having come to the conclusion that he'd had his share of joy and sorrow, Orvil decided that the best thing for him to do was to leave. That's just what he did one morning in May 1982, between the short and the long rainy seasons. He now felt insignificant in a world in which he had always been powerless. Powerless, but a son of the gods. Blind, but steady on the raging waters, in the turmoil and the great hurricane of life. His impotence had lately been transformed into weariness. He no longer had the strength to wait for his two children to return from God knows where. He no longer had the strength to call the gods. Of this he was certain.

He wanted to join them. Where they were. Be by their side. Fall asleep at their feet. Feel their hands on his wounds. Return to *Guinée*. To the early days of the sea. To the lights, the ones you can see in the *devant jour*, those that you can't see in the storms at night, those in the hearts of the trees and plants, the pristine and intact light of the *bon ange*, the same, always, the only.

He was crippled with pain and was no longer able to devote himself to the labors whose roughness and monotony nonetheless brought him a form of peace and the feeling of still being rooted in the soil or gliding over the current. He walked slowly, stubborn as the donkeys who carry out a task with strain and caution. His jaw fell open because of gums that had receded over the years. He was nothing but skin and bones, like death wanted to carry him away light as a child, bare as an angel.

On the eve of the day when he had chosen to leave, Orvil fell asleep calmly, and upon waking called Ermancia for the coffee that he drank thick and sweet *au rapadou*. He sipped it while sitting at the entrance of his hut, waiting for everyone's greetings: "How was the night? *Figi a fré papa?* You're looking well? *Kouman kò a yé?*" The round of greetings had barely ended when Orvil asked Ermancia, with authority and tenderness, to draw him a bath. Ermancia placed the white enameled basin, lined with blue, in the sun and crushed up orange tree leaves, *ti baume,* and soursop. Wrapped up in a threadbare woolen blanket, Orvil waited, sipping the last drops of coffee that filled his mouth with a lukewarm sweetness. Once the bathwater was warm, Ermancia helped him take off his clothes, sit down in the basin, and vigorously, with her right hand, rubbed his back, chest, and stomach with soap.

Then she bent the palm of her left hand to collect the water that she then poured on Orvil's chest, stomach, and back, rinsing him slowly. Sweetly. With infinite tenderness. Singing him a song he loved. And he, twenty years her senior, he who could have been her father, wanted to call her Mother. As men here tend to do when they really give in. It was the only way for him to tell her that he had lived life with something good, sweet, and strong beside him. "You know, I'm leaving today. *Mwen pralé.*" And when she told him to stop talking nonsense, she told him, really, that even if his other women had come to the fence one day to insult her, it did not matter. He thanked her without saying so for the two children who were not her own and to whom Ermancia regularly sent rice, vegetables, and money as though they were her own flesh. When he repeated for the third time, "I am going away, *Sia. Mwen pralé,*" Ermancia told him, openly, that he'd been beaten down by his worries, the stingy sea, the abandoned land. By Olmène, who had never returned. By Léosthène, so far away. By Fénelon too. But that, even if the land did not give as much and the sea neither, she and Dieudonné had gotten by, with the bread oven and her small business at the stall. Orvil did not respond.

After the bath, he walked barefoot, with slow, measured steps, taking in the landscape, his body collapsing under the wind. Relieved by having nothing else to do in these moments but contemplate the world and let himself be invaded by its light. He had suffered the burning of the sun on the hard blue of the sea, its unrelenting bite on the knotty paths of the Lavandou and Peletier Mornes. He had done his time. He sang, in a whisper, a song he learned from Bonal, his father, who learned it from his own father, and he traced it back to Dieunor, the *franginen* forefather, who said that it was necessary to pass it down and let it go before leaving. But pass it down to whom?

Orvil stopped his pained stride and found himself saying out loud: "I did my duty. I led this *lakou* with a firm and just hand. I do not know how much I have protected each of the *chrétiens vivants* of this *lakou* against the night, the evil spirits, and the shadows within us. Yet someone must continue. Maintain the blood. As long as the *lwas* are there, there will be something to give. To ourselves, to others. All I know, I learned by feeding each other, by giving. Léosthène won't return, Fénelon cannot. No, he cannot and must not. Dieudonné, when the time comes, will take over. That's all. It's time for me to leave…" And Orvil continued to walk. He had always savored this time on the paths. Never lost. Suddenly, under the weakness of his body, an unexpected strength unburdened his steps.

At the end of his walk, he leaned his chair against the imposing *mapou* and began to sing again. He did not reply to the greetings of the men who were returning from fishing. To those returning from the lands. To the women preparing the meal. To those who were leaving to do laundry in the river. We thought that Orvil was starting to lose his mind. At the strike of three, Ermancia yelled for him, only to find his head bent over his chest, his arms dangling, his hat on the floor. Orvil was already a limp rag, barely warm.

Cilianise was on the *Dieu très haut* bus, sitting on one of the eight benches occupied by fifty-six *chrétiens-vivant* who were on their way to Baudelet, and lent a distracted ear to the community radio. The driver shrieked, rocking beneath the weight of three goats and six chickens tied together by their feet and two other goats atop the vehicle, that the sky was wearing its mask of clouds and that they had to go fast, *pressé, pressé*. The crew got going in its usual commotion. And between the sound of the engine, the chattering, and the cries of the animals, the radio rang out his long list of messages: "Roselène, who lives in Périchon, *pas bliyé*, don't forget, Macéna is waiting for you at the Carrefour de Ti Pistache for the commission." "André, Ismena has a high fever and will not come to the market today, but tomorrow, God willing." "Cilianise, who lives in Anse Bleue, come back immediately, *pa mizé*, Orvil *malade grave*." Cilianise could hardly make the connection between her name, which came out of the front of the truck, and herself. When she finally understood that it was for her, she let out a piercing cry and was seized by convulsions. The fifty-six passengers helped her carry her grief to her destination.

With Cilianise, Ermancia, and Dieudonné, we helped Orvil's soul depart intact. We helped it to not disseminate everywhere. To not leave any trace. In his hut, in the trees, in the gardens or the nearby rivers. To go intact toward its true death. We did all that was necessary for Orvil to leave quietly and calmly. A *hougan*, led by Érilien, helped Agwé, his *mèt tèt*, let go of him. Ermancia cut his nails and hair, which she kept in two vials, and told him her messages for the Invisibles: "Ask them to tell you where Olmène is, *tanpri*. When you find her, tell her in a dream that I love her. That I have never forgotten her. And then, watch over us. Over our gardens. Over our animals. Over our commerce. Over our boats."

It was Father André, Father Bonin's successor, who presided over the funeral. The man with the black hat and thick glasses, wishing to indigenize the clergy, had sent us Father André, who sometimes cleaned his gun right in front the presbytery. A way to say that he had his eyes on us and would send reports to the priests more powerful than him—who, in turn, would hand them over to the man with the black hat and thick glasses—reports on our possible disobedience. It was the only thing that mattered to him. We never gave him the opportunity to make such reports. Nor to kill any of us. Why had he joined the Holy Order? We never knew. Perhaps he just wanted to never go hungry, never have to worry about tomorrow, to be above earthly creatures like us. None of these questions stopped us from smiling at him, from pleasing him with the produce of our *jardins* and the few poultry of our coops, and from secretly watching him.

Father André was not the least bit surprised to find us on the road to Anse Bleue, zigzagging, turning back, going from one side to the other with Orvil's coffin, to make him lose his way. To rid him of any desire to return to visit us before he had finished his journey. Zigzagging, retracing our steps, going from one side to the other, we had erased our own footprints and we were as incapable as Orvil of going back.

Ilménèse and Cilianise took over and cajoled the Invisibles, awaiting their calls, messages, and lessons. Dieudonné still wasn't ready.

With Orvil's death, all of Anse Bleue had the feeling that this was a world that was receding. The old world. That Orvil had left us in an even greater confusion and disorder slithering like Mary Magdalene's serpent, spreading out like a contagious disease.

30.

Dieudonné met Philomène Florival for the first time on the road near Roseaux, one day when he was going toward the thick brush of Nan Pikan, despite the ban by the health authorities, to sell one of the last indigenous piglets of Anse Bleue to a *hougan*. Dieudonné did not notice Philomène immediately, but rather when she was about to pass him near the cattle market. And, despite her calm demeanor and the conservative clothes she wore as she stood beside her mother, Dieudonné noticed her young honeypot body. Watching her out of the corner of his eye, he would have sworn on what he held most dear that Erzuli Fréda herself slept inside Philomène's eyes. She was sleeping, but she was there, sensual and capricious. Dieudonné was sure of it.

They crossed paths a second time at the Frétillon's shop in Baudelet. She was choosing colored buttons from glass jars for dresses that her mother sewed from dawn to dusk, pedaling on an old Singer machine: "A dozen big yellow buttons, *tanpri*, two dozen small white buttons, six blue buttons, six red buttons, *mési*." When she turned to leave the shop, Philomène smiled at Dieudonné and left as though she was bathed in molasses. Yet she was not like those young women in Baudelet who now wore heels so tall they could hardly walk. No, Philomène had chosen to remain as the good Lord had made her, round and juicy like a mango. She didn't powder her face, nor did she put polish on her nails or red on her lips, and she had none of those dresses that stopped above the knee and sealed the real *jeunesses* of today's girls. But, without even noticing it, she had, solely by the power of her presence, brought the sun with her into the shop and left Dieudonné, stunned, stuck there like a stake in the ground.

The third time he saw Philomène, on Good Friday, she was dressed in all white, a missal in her hand, a scarf tied round her head as she returned, tired from having gone through the fourteen stations of the cross. Despite her loose clothing, Dieudonné could see buttocks and nipples that would captivate even the wisest angels in God's domain. He was convinced that, beneath her holy air, always by her mother's side, always saying: "Yes, sir." "I beg your pardon?" "Tomorrow, God willing." Eyes lowered, she taunted him. Not like a *jeunesse*, oh no, but like a tease, a *riseuse*. Yes, that's right, she was taunting him, Dieudonné Dorival. He swore to Fanol and Ézéchiel that he would have her and that she would be his wife. They told him he was kidding himself and that such a girl was too fine for his peasant's mouth.

We saw Dieudonné borrow money from Fénelon, buy a large sack of rice, which he sold at a profit near Ermancia's stall, cut trees on abandoned land to make coal, and, thanks to the profits on all these sales and the money Léosthène sent, open the first *borlette** between Ti Pistache, Anse Bleue, and Roseaux. Dieudonné now spent a good part of the day with his ear glued to the post to hear that day's numbers. He had come to know the *Tchala* by his fingertips, the great book on the interpretation of dreams, which assigns a number to each of them. This skill made him a reputation far beyond Anse Bleue. It was enough for the client to tell what he had seen behind his eyelids the night before: "I ran, chased by a three-horned ox, and fell, breaking my little toe." Dieudonné, without hesitation, replied, "Fourteen for the three-horned ox, twenty-two for the fall, and fifty-three for the broken toe." Between customers, he played dominoes on the table set up for that purpose in front of his *borlette*. Where men gathered who, tired of the earth and disappointed by the sea, awaited envelopes from Miami, the Bahamas, Guadeloupe, or Turk and Caicos, along with the exhilarating and marvelous luck of numbers, before falling asleep toward new dreams.

Dieudonné saved so much money that one morning he stopped Philomène on the road to Ti Pistache and offered her three mints that she accepted with a laugh. And, at the end of a sunless afternoon in September, he asked permission for a little indecency. Then she took him by the hand to an isolated hut not far from Ti Pistache. With the other wandering hand, she guided him between her powerful and chubby thighs. She clung to his back, and Dieudonné sunk deep inside her, letting out a long moan. Dieudonné did not know where Philomène's sweet fury came from. No, he didn't know. But he took advantage of it as a hungry man picks up crumbs under a table. All the crumbs.

With the speed of a madman Dieudonné built a hut next to his grandmother's and, once the door and the windows were installed, Ermancia and Cilianise saw a young woman arrive, three months pregnant.

Dieudonné would often take Philomène, willing and silent, in that same glowing vertigo. In Philomène he found several women, all women, the sweet, the courageous, and the serene. And Dieudonné wanted them all. Happiness filled the hut. All of it. And then the children were born and days passed, seemingly alike, boredom gnawing at them from within. Then Philomène spent most of her days threading a needle, then later pedaling on the

Singer machine that she had inherited from her mother. At night she opened herself obediently to Dieudonné's seed. A seed that he also shared with some young negresses, in the villages further inland. Philomène, the first of his wives, raised no fewer than two sons and two daughters. Her youngest boy died at birth and the second daughter from malaria that had been mistreated. No one knew the exact color and shape of those borne of other wombs.

Some women were angry with Philomène. Others even wanted her dead. By accident or illness. One, whom Dieudonné had given two children, attacked her not far from the market, shouting threats against she whose bread she had taken from their mouth. In a moment of rage, Philomène grabbed her dress and pulled it so forcefully that the fabric tore, exposing her neck and two breasts to the outcries of the women and onlookers.

Another, more daring than all the others, decided to come as far as Anse Bleue. Cilianise helped Philomène beat back the intruder. She grabbed the heavy pocket that was her belly and advanced like there was a hurricane in her blouse, the color and patterns clashing with her skirt and the hair that she hadn't combed. The intruder fled and was never heard from again.

Noting that no injuries, accidents nor illnesses were reaching Philomène, another woman, who thought herself powerful, wanted to lend a helping hand to fate by sprinkling one of the paths that Philomène frequented, just before she passed, with a powder meant to swell her legs so much that she would die in atrocious pain. The *matelote* abandoned the struggle when Philomène, standing on legs long like palm trees, was pregnant again by Dieudonné and gave birth to Éliphète and, eleven months later, Cétoute Olmène Thérèse.

31.

*Someone killed me. I am sure. It is because of this pain that persists around my neck. I'm sure, I do not doubt it any more. Someone killed me before escaping to the* bayahondes *off in the hills. I am Cétoute Olmène Thérèse, the youngest daughter of Philomène Florival and Dieudonné Dorival.*

*Olmène because Dieudonné, my father, wanted his mother to live again in me. He had seen her in a dream three days before my birth. They say I have her eyes and her smile. Dieudonné, my father, wanted me to replace the dream woman who came down the long ladder hanging from the clouds. I always felt the lack of this link in the chain. A fault between me and eternity. I always felt that throughout my life I had stood at the edge of a precipice. That a lugubrious and black wind blew at my back.*

*Thérèse because my mother, Philomène, had never forgotten the story of the life of Thérèse d'Avila, God's madwoman, that she'd been told at Catechism. She did not want me to be crazy, but filled with the bright lights that she'd extinguished by settling in Anse Bleue.*

*Cétoute, like* "c'est tout," *"that's all," because my mother Philomène wanted nothing more than for me to be the last. In order not to keep the promise of ten or fifteen children buried in the depths of the wombs of women here.*

*I'm just called Cétoute. The one whom people have grown accustomed to not seeing. Came too late. In a tired belly, already committed to a certain sterility. In this oblivion, I made a wild and unrestrained life for myself, entrusting all my madness to the sea. It was before Jimmy. Before school. Before the plane and the fire.*

*And here I am cast down on the sand. Before the eyes of an entire village. Four men carry me on this white sheet. Each one holds one corner. And here I am, balancing at the mercy of their steps, from one side to the other.*

*Early in the morning, once she had coffee, my mother lay her feet quietly along the black lace of the seaweed, sighed, and then sat down, legs spread like a pregnant cow, and waited. What was she waiting for? I will never know. But, like her, I resolved myself to keep my eyes open. To surprise what the sea hides under her dress of salt and water. The frothy mysteries and damp and purple dreams of my mother Philomène. And it's by scrutinizing the sky, questioning the ocean, my soul tortured by their strangeness, that I have learned to love the extravagance, the turbulence, and the beauty of the world.*

*With Altagrâce, my sister, Éliphète, my brother, this fondness for water began very early. Between the work in the house and the work in the fields, we try to swim by imitating the frantic movements of dogs treading in the water. We knead the sand in our hands to make gray bread, mud huts. Even when our fingers are numb and we chatter our teeth, we still demand the spectacles of sparks and mirrors from the sea. Often we lay out on the sand, the sea licks our feet and we laugh with rainbows in our eyes and large birds perched on our hands. In the evening, we fall asleep, body, face, and hands frosted with salt.*

*Abner is not afraid of anything. One evening, he decided to show me the night despite the protests of my father and mother, who begged him to return. Outside, the screeching of the insects was unleashed. I liked seeing the* coucouyes★ *fly like tiny stars. I loved the voluptuous blanket of the night. I am in the night as in the flesh of Philomène. And then one day I felt the cold of the moon wash over my belly, the belly of a girl, like a bath, I never forgot it.*

*Abner is much bigger than any of us. He is the only one to accompany me in the night. To take these moon baths with me. To taste the wild beauty, the violent mystery of the night.*

32.

Father Lucien was a native of the Cayes. He replaced Father André on one July morning. Father Lucien was from the Petite Église, which did not want to receive orders from the Grande Église nor from the Palais. Wandering with faith and obstinacy throughout the region, he met the faithful at home, in their *jardins*, their shops, or their *borlettes*. A way for him to extend, throughout the five surrounding villages, the tentacles of the party of the Destitute, which was beginning to take shape. And, destitute as we were, we were their favorite target.

One Saturday in December, Father Lucien was preparing to receive militants from Port-au-Prince for an important meeting. Fanol and Ézéchiel had gone to meet them, taking paths through the fields to avoid Roseaux, and above all Fenelon. We found out after the fact, but we hadn't been at all surprised. We had all noticed how Fanol and Ézéchiel's eyes shined for the past few months, with the excitement of children contemplating their dreams. Cilianise hadn't missed this sudden rise of fervor either. We watched them and they knew it.

Once this mission had been completed, Fanol and Ézéchiel did all they could to convince Dieudonné, Oxéna, and Cilianise to accompany them to a meeting at the presbytery. Yvnel, meanwhile, adamantly refused.

"Who wants to see us?" asked Dieudonné, skeptical.

"Yes, who?" added Yvnel.

"Honest men and women."

Dieudonné and Oxéna burst out laughing.

"Have you ever met honest politicians?"

"Yes. Those over there."

"That's it, that's it. Give us some *clairin* and make us cry by getting us to sway to the sound of music. The country is for you, *péyi a sé pou ou*, do with it what you want! *É yan é yan…*"

But their arguments ended up melting our thick armor of mistrust. Dieudonné, Oxéna, and Cilianise had given in and agreed to join Fanol and Ézéchiel, who, listening to Father Lucien for almost three years, had learned to no longer want that life we'd been given, we who have been poor since the beginning of time. With the help of two German volunteers, Father Lucien built two fountains between Roseaux and Anse Bleue, expanded the school and clinic, and built a soccer field. We stood by the fountains, at the school, and at the dispensary, we stood by football the pitch, and at the same time, we stood by Father Lucien, who was definitively one of us. We therefore agreed to remain silent, so that the news would not reach the ears of Fénelon or Toufik Békri.

And then, with Father Lucien's sermons urging, the radios too, we all ended up resenting the man with the black hat and thick glasses. His friends, his men in blue uniforms, his accomplices, people whom, after all, we did not know. In a room next to the presbytery, Father Lucien greeted all those present, other monks and nuns of the Petite Église, agronomists and people with notebooks under their arms, tape recorders and glasses who spoke volumes about their desire to know us better than we knew ourselves. Nothing about us should escape them. They were attentive and excessively humble. Then we played the game of those who were being watched and pretended not to be.

Father Lucien invited us all to sit in a circle, and the newcomers sat down among us. Dieudonné, Oxéna, and Cilianise thought up a strategy. One more. We were ready to defend ourselves against this new assault. To pretend to lend ourselves to it in order to stop it. To pretend to listen to them, but to hear only a distant refrain. At this game, there is no one better at it than us. And Father Lucien knew it. So he went to extraordinary lengths to speak Creole slowly and with a peasant accent, inflections that belonged to us. He went over the top. So much so that it became at once credible and unnatural, blurring our mistrust in a large dark cloud.

Packed shoulder to shoulder, we drank a good part of the words of the militants of the party of the Destitute who, with their notes and their notebooks, their great faith and their bare feet in dusty sandals, described to us, behind their glasses, happiness of a rare extravagance. The one that the Mésidors and the Frétillons, and all those who resemble them, had never let us see. They launched into fierce tirades against those who had taken away our pigs to sell us others, frail and more expensive, of blond princes who had come from the United States. Against those who had suffocated us with taxes and fees of all kinds. Those who had killed all our small-scale commerce, leaving us no choice but to cut the trees.

The powerful words, magic, melted our thick armor of doubts. When they told us that change was on its way and that soon the pain would not only disappear, but would give way to the the rise of hope, we believed it. For a few seconds. Weeks, even months. We believed it. Who knows why, but we believed it. Especially what, for days, weeks and months, Fanol and Ézéchiel had repeated to us over and over, that with the party of the Destitute we could finally choose our own destiny. Carried, like them, along a road with turns and detours we thought we foresaw, we moved forward only to fall backward. The road would only be clear to us afterward. Once the die was cast. Long after.

A few weeks later, under the guise of a large public prayer meeting, there was a gathering in the square in Baudelet, under the noses of the soldiers and men in blue. The promise of the happiness to come was magnified tenfold by a megaphone. The songs to Jesus, God, Mary, and all the saints echoed in our ears and we were electrified. Never had Cilianise spoken out so much. Little Altagrâce, the youngest of Dieudonné and Philomène, too. And the voices of the priests, emboldened by the growing enthusiasm of the crowd, threw out promises like they were bulls roaring. Madame Frétillon looked at us in terror, and summoned her brother to go look in on this unprecedented event: the awakening of the peasants. Upon his arrival, Toufik Békri didn't flinch, knowing that the march against the party of the Destitute was already ready. He reassured her: "Wait a bit and you'll see!"

That same day, in fact, the party of the Rich had decided to hold a meeting a block away in order to distribute food. Many of us couldn't resist the lure of bags of *riz Miami*, *farine France*, and big cans of powdered milk. The shops and houses of Baudelet quickly closed their doors. As far back as any man—or woman—could remember, nobody had ever seen such a torrent in the city. Those who looked at us, from behind their blinds or drawn curtains, did so with astonishment, as if they were seeing us for the first time. Because of the years of mistrust and misery that had become so encrusted on our faces. And that made us look at the world with an acute curiosity. That made us look at it, often, with a malice rivaling our hunger. They did not recognize us.

The idlers, the street vendors, the porters, they all joined us. Women yelled in the scramble as they tried to catch a bag of rice. Fanol and Ézéchiel got away with a sack each, Cilianise a big can of powdered milk. Altagrâce and other children were stepped on when they opened their hands to collect the flour that came out of bags torn open by the unleashed crowd. Everything became frenzied. The distribution turned into a riot. Fights broke out… The wave of the hungry, we were in it, swept around the trucks. And soon the women had their headscarves torn off and the men with their shirts ripped, their hair sprinkled with rice, their faces white with powdered milk.

Overwhelmed by the turn of events, frightened, the militia fired into the crowd. One. Two. Three bursts. Two men and one child were killed instantly by the bullets. Women fainted in the rush that followed. Then we emerged on the main road, for the first time without it being for a *rara*.★ Without a *roi*. Without *drapeaux*.★ Without *majò jon*.★ Without *vaccines*★ and without drums. Just us. Bare hands. Bare feet. Terrified eyes. Like a mob from the afterlife. The last *taps-taps*★ sped off, their passengers crammed together on the benches. We kept going until the night, like a big mouth, devoured the road. We looted the shops and robbed the rare passersby who had lingered. We set fires and everything in our path burned.

And then we went home late in the night, among the shadows, to listen, ears to the transistors, to the radio broadcasts from Port-au-Prince shouting that the land couldn't offer enough. And that the gods were still thirsty. And that in Baudelet there had been some blunders and bloodshed. For the first time, they spoke of us in Port-au-Prince, as they soon would of a dozen other cities.

So, very quickly, in one night, it was over. Because this stillness had to shatter. Let the door of expectations be forced open with a brutal blow. New forces had mingled with the night and had converted it to the cause of the Destitute and those who wished to be innocent. Port-au-Prince, the great city, burned in a quiet surge. The flames, high and red, rose in plumes like blossoming flowers. The machetes blazed. The songs faded and died in a din of syllables. Misfortune seemed to want to break the night's teeth. And those who had born it bumped into their own shadows. We heard them screaming the name of their mothers, while the innocents smashed bottles on their heads, chased them, and they fell under the rage of cutlasses with blunt edges. Bodies were burned alive with tires firmly tied around their necks, and old women accused of witch-craft, lynched here and there. The night had been long, pierced by calls of *conch lambi*★ riddled with muffled gusts. And the whole thing filled our chests like a hot rum.

In Anse Bleue, we woke up, that morning of February 1986, to the same shimmer of the first rays of sun above the water, the same crow of the roosters, the same harshness of ordinary days. Just a little more attentive to the expectation of that promised happiness. But we did not hope anymore. Ermancia had the same dream of flames surrounding her son Fénelon. Dieudonné decided to light up the *liminin* for the *lwas*.

33.

Standing in front of the Frétillons' shop with the closed shutters, Fénelon opened his eyes in disbelief when a friend told him that the family of the man with black hat and thick glasses had left in the middle of the night. Fénelon had left Roseaux early in the morning and was going to the base in Baudelet to receive instructions from the militia leader, not knowing that Toufik Békri had crossed the border in the middle of the night. Nor that Tertulien Mésidor was already in hiding and that, disguised as a woman, he was getting reading to leave at any moment, to follow the same route in the night. Neither of them had warned him. Nobody.

"That's not true!" Fénelon cried out to the friend who told him the news, discretely, so that he could take cover. "It is impossible," added an incredulous Fénelon, who didn't doubt for a second that the crowd was already watching him.

A few weeks ago, the news of the debacle had spread and reached Baudelet. Fénelon had simply decided to not listen to the radio. Not to lend an ear to this misleading propaganda. To these subversive and, above all, untrue words. He had even locked up, after beating them to a pulp, two regulars at the *borlette,* who, under pretext of listening to the winning numbers, had been bouncing with anticipation in front of him, in plain sight, to hear news of the fall, the debacle. Recalling the incident, Fénelon went so far as to whisper to himself: "That's right. I beat them to a pulp. A lesson to discourage all who would think of doing what they did." Perhaps he spoke to himself to ignore the rumor that was growing behind his back. Around him. That of the silent crowd which soon was going to be his entourage. The younger men were already intoxicated by the magnetizing smells of that morning's storm. The lips of a young mechanic quivered. He was a militant in the party of the Destitute. Coming from Port-au-Prince, he had never had enough to eat. His violence was cast in pure metal. He was one of those who wanted to cut off a few thousand filthy heads in public squares. And now a filthy head appeared before him. A real filthy head. At that moment, in the party of the Destitute, they had no time to forgive. Forgive, right away, right now, on the spot, with hatred hot like a heart in your hand? No, they could not. Because hatred, she made you feel good inside. She comforted like faith in God. They did not have time to judge. They were killing.

Someone in the crowd calls Fénelon by name. And for the first time, the name he had always known takes on a new sound. This name slowly invades his chest, his whole body, penetrates the depths of his life and gives him a weight he did not know until then. As if his whole life was suddenly inside that moment and in those syllables. The voice adds:

"Fénelon, you're going to die!"

A group of men emerged from the market and blocked him. The crowd had grown in rage and in number because prices had been rising for some time, because the drought had been rough. Because children had died of dengue fever, lack of care. And Fénelon had been sowing fear inside of them for years. A vast anger sleeping in each of these men, each of these women, it overwhelmed them. They wanted to extract that anger like a loose tooth.

Father Lucien, feeling the beast grow inside of every man, every woman, to the point of making of a single beast of the whole crowd, interrupted and cried out: "Let he among you that is without sin cast the first stone!" The first stone came from a stall on the left and hit Fénelon straight in the chest. A blow that could take out a donkey. In shock, Fénelon lost his balance. While trying to get up, a second shot kept him on the ground. The insults rained down from all sides, at the same time as the stones. In the crowd, some even laughed. An indecent, cruel laugh, capable of driving back the sun. But it was still there, the sun, and Fénelon could not quite see it through the blood that stuck to his lashes.

Fénelon is dazed. He does not understand. He is pulled from all sides. From the right. From the left. Forward. Backward. His big blue shirt is torn. Two buttons have already popped off. Fénelon wipes the blood off his face, his chest. Fénelon trembles. He is afraid. When the second shot hits him in the face, his sight is blurred. He feels that the countdown has begun. He is going toward his death. The pain is atrocious. The flowing blood mixes with the sweat and blinds him. People are approaching from all sides. Someone strikes a drum, then an impromptu song rises from chests and mixes with shouts, the songs of the truckers, the porters, the peasants who have just arrived from the *jardins*, the merchants from the stalls. Blood makes you want to hit harder. People are elbowing to be in the front row. And then the blows come down vigorously. Everyone is crowding around Fénelon and everyone would like to be part of this big party and offer a blow. He receives one so hard that he thinks his skull will burst. Then, mustering whatever strength he had left, Fenelon made a strange decision, to get up and go forward.

Skull busted and blood running down his neck. Where was he going? He did not know it himself. The time to launch a counter attack that would enable him to breach the seven circles of this stubborn and terrible army had long since passed. As had the chance to call Toufik Békri to his aide. No, he would not run away. He would put one foot after the other, a way not to die on his knees, he who had humiliated so many men and women for miles around.

A dark spot appears on the crotch of his pants. The crowd laughs, plugs their noses and insults him more. Fénelon stammers and speaks like a child. Snot and blood flow from his nose. They tell him it hasn't even started.

And then someone comes with a rope. They tie it up like for the pigs they hang from the top of the trucks. When the machete cuts his right shoulder, there was nothing else he could do. Fénelon falls, and in his fall he hits the feet of a young peasant, who, with a blow of his boot, breaks his shoulder blade. His sight blurs completely. Just in time for Fénelon to see the blade of the machete that cuts off his foot. His flesh, his bones, his skull, and his heart are nothing but a bloody pile in the mud. The earth herself seems to drink his blood.

"Let him have it."

Then three men run for a tire. The mechanic grabs a block of cement which he drops with little thought on Fénelon's skull.

The crowd moves in on the corpse and, unable to end the rampage, insults Fénelon. The mechanic slides a used tire around his body. The smell of gasoline rises and soon, too, that of the body and the tire as they burn.

The news reached Ermancia a few hours later. Ermancia collapsed for days to mourn her son, letting herself go like someone drowning in water, gulping the salt of her tears. Letting herself be gnawed by the vermin of the sweet and terrifying memories of this son. Yes, terrifying memories. Muddled and mixed up without end…She doesn't move for hours, frozen like the the corpse of the son she loved no matter what. Out of a mother's blind and unjust love. "Why Fénelon," she repeated to herself. "Why him and not Toufik and not Tertulien? Why my son? And only my son?" The death of Dorcélien, a few days later, burned alive with his tire collar firmly attached to his neck, strengthened her bitterness and rage against the world as it was.

Ermancia would have faded away, like a drawing that gets erased, had Dieudonné not given her four grandchildren: two sons and two daughters. She died in peace a few years after the birth of Cétoute, the very last one. Cétoute resembled Olmène as two drops of water do each other. The resemblance did not replace Olmène's absence or Fénelon's death. But the resemblance consoled her.

34.

*Often, in order to forget that in Anse Bleue life puts two anchors at your feet, I came to the shore to watch the waves build up and fall apart, to breathe through each of my pores, and to soak myself in iodine and kelp, the acrid scents of the sea that leave a strange bite on the soul.*

*Even when the sea became that gleaming plate, spread out on the horizon, I left the burned inlands to look at her until I blinked, until I was blinded.*

*Even when the* nordé *thundered three days and nights in a row, I listened in order to be turned upside down, her voice shattering the rocks, I tasted her salty breath on my face, again and again.*

*And then one year, October came to an end, my childhood with it. I knew it, too, when a wound, unknown to me until then, bled the afternoon before the hurricane. I felt very funny. I was hot. I was cold. At the sight of the blood flowing down my thighs, I leaned over to see the source of this injury. After that day, my sea dreams were disturbed by the distant sound of high heels, very beautiful, well made-up women, like on the television in the school principal's office, Headmaster Émile. I now know how boys are made. I also know the prominent thing planted right in the middle of their bodies. I know I have a body made to fit theirs…*

*I love the sea, its mystery. Watching the sea, I always thought that I would one day bring up the entire array of those who sleep in the hollowness of her womb on beds of algae and coral. Those in the waterways, their ocean route to the distant Guinée with Agwé, Simbi, and Lasirenn escorting them.*

*My father said that all the voices of the Ancestors and the Dead, even those who arrived in the holds of ships long ago, still blow in the ocean forest, sometimes ascend to the surface of the waters like words mixed with the night. In the holds, one could not tell day from night. None of us knew whether the ship was heading toward the horizon or if it was about to sink into the depths of the water. We didn't pinch our noses because of the vomit and didn't even avoid the defecations. A cry, a song, and tears, came to pierce the uninterrupted murmur of hundreds of men, shoulder to shoulder.*

*My father said that sailors, not knowing how to distinguish dreams from exhaustion, lost their minds. He often said that boats were sailing toward death, believing it was on the horizon. A spot tossed on the fury* of the waves, burnt by salt, struck by the sun to the point of vertigo. The men saw a flock of birds pass in the sky, and thought they heard in their cries the voices of Lasirenn, Agwé, and Labalenn. They were going to die with the sun in the other half of the sky.

Mother and Cilianise, they were convinced that I could see what the others did not see. That I had the gift of vision. But I was only looking for the face of Olmène, my grandmother, to fill the void between me and the dark matter of the world. And I believed in her appearance, and I still do. As I believe in the mystery of the Immaculate Conception, in the seven faces of Aunt Cilianise's Ogou, or in the fact that every body immersed in water is pushed upward…At school, Headmaster Émile took three long days to explain it to us. I believe in all this and much more.

Dieudonné wanted Abner, Éliphète, Altagrâce, and I to go to the little school in Roseaux and later to the big school in Baudelet. He hadn't had the chance. I, the last, took advantage of their progress and stayed longer than the others at the big school. But Abner remained longer than any of us. I remember one day he even came back from night class given by benevolent people whose names he did not tell us. Two months later, he proposed that our father Dieudonné enroll in a literacy course.

One afternoon, my father came in with a pencil, a book, a notebook under his arm, and named Altagrâce his teacher. For months we listened to Altagrâce, who had him repeat in front of the hut: "M-A-N, MAN, G-O, GO, MANGO." Despite the laughter of the children who, in the early days, formed a joyous and curious circle around the hut, chanting the alphabet with him, Abner helped our father keep going. And my father learned to decipher the beautiful secrets of words. I was even surprised by him once or twice, when he wanted to go faster than the speed of light, to invent new words, like his children before him. He seemed so fragile that one *night, out of my love for him, I wept. But I was already on the other side. I was in a foreign land.*

*Abner has a quick mind. His intelligence, Abner uses it to tell us as soon as possible, before any of us, what to do. In all circumstances. Perhaps he doesn't even formulate the answers in his head. They are there, in his blood, waiting.*

35.

After all these years of struggle, of persistence, of resistance, the party of the Destitute ended up with the wind in its sails. So much so that on the day when the prophet, the leader of the party, was to visit Baudelet, we woke up in the night and went into the streets with torches, hearts beating. We were led by a curiosity entirely new to us. For once, we wanted to know.

We are among the first and we sit in the rows close to the platform. If the most zealous were the militants of the Petite Église, the most numerous were the beggars, the idlers, and especially the young, who would have done anything to be there. We had goose bumps, our eyes shined, our lips quivered. The others, those who had not been touched by grace, said to themselves that if they could not get dressed, wear proper shoes, or eat their fill, at least they could afford an exceptional spectacle, and a free one to boot, that, who knows, might offer some entertainment. The crowd was fascinated and shouted the name of the prophet, and we shouted it with all the strength of our lungs "*Profit, papa, chief nou.*" Cilianise had stuck a picture of the prophet to her

chest, as had her two sons Fanol and Ézéchiel. Oxéna and Dieudonné lifted their arms to heaven at the prophet's every word, he
who skillfully blended the the honey with the *piment-bouc*, the
sharp blade of the knife with the softest down. We greedily swallowed the words coming out of this mouth, which, like ours,
said everything by saying almost nothing at all. How strong he
was, the prophet! The parable of the stone that flowed softly in the
water and was going to have to know the pain and suffering of the
one who burns in the sun concluded the meeting in an apotheosis.

After the meeting, the crowd slowly dispersed. Some of them,
like Cilianise, cried out their joy alone or in groups. Some of
the youth improvised a band with drums and *vaccines* and everyone began dancing like at the carnival. Others advanced in
silence, like Oxéna. Some, like Dieudonné, tried with difficulty
to sober themselves up a little more with each step, to return
to their senses. Many, like Fanol and Ézéchiel, did not want to
free themselves from the intoxication the prophet had thrown
them into. All of us struggled to return to the pettiness and
monotony of our daily lives. Something had narrowed our gaze.
Burned our blood.

And we wanted to hold onto this thing as long as possible. And
we fostered it, despite the dead and the wounded, until the prophet
was in the Palais National. But once in the Palais National, the
prophet had turned into something that looked uncannily like the
man with a black hat and thick glasses. The legend that the seat
was cursed held true. It was enough to sit on it to be mounted
by a lawless, faithless god. As the months passed, the resemblance
became even more striking. The mask no longer hid the face of

the man with black hat and thick glasses. The prophet departed and returned under American escort. With the second occupation, the peace that was not peace merged into a war that couldn't hatch. We had no more *dokos* to take refuge in. Even the *dokos* in our heads had retreated. We were even more naked than our ancestor Bonal. Gran Bwa Îlé seemed powerless to guide our steps. The disaster became banal.

Like many of those who had made a fortune under the man with a black hat and thick glasses, Madame Frétillon became untouchable and a made herself an indispensable advisor to the prophet. Go figure! The powerful Madame Frétillon multiplied her earnings again, while her brother, Toufik Békri, got secret security protection from the Palais. They gathered round the great banquet tables for feasts and left us with our dreams of pebbles that would glide in the freshness of rivers running through green groves. When Madame Frétillon returned to Baudelet under the cover of the Church of the Poor, to organize a big prayer meeting, we asked ourselves the same questions that Orvil had upon Bonal's death, the same questions that Ermancia had upon Fénelon's. Questions about the hunter and the prey, those who crush and those who are crushed. About those who are poor from the start and will remain poor until the trumpets of Judgement Day resound. But we closed our eyes and prayed and sang with a fervor that amazed the authorities who, though new, were also old. We prayed with lumps in our throats and the taste of the dream in our mouths, a ginger candy that refused to dissolve.

Dieudonné returned to the bread oven and worked twice as hard, searching for the wood that left charred skeletons of trees at the top of the hills each day. He deserted the land and his outings to sea became less frequent. Yvnel grew upset with the thankless land he was breaking his back over, under a sun that stabbed at his back with lashes of fire. Philomène, on the other hand, no longer sewed, she liked to kneel, her fingers in pain from rosaries done with the charismatic nuns, praying for the help of Notre-Dame du Perpétuel Secours, the patroness of Haiti.

Altagrâce helped Cilianise to the store and, together as two accomplices, they took care of every detail to prepare the service for the wedding of Cilianise and Ogou. As he had learned from his father, who had learned from his grandfather Bonal, Dieudonné fasted, lay down right on the ground in order to hear the heart beat of the earth, and abstained from words and flesh in order to prepare for Ogou's arrival at this extravagant wedding.

36.

*Aunt Cilianise's marriage to Ogou was the most beautiful party of my childhood. Aunt Cilianise had smoldered with her love for Ogou for a long time. A long time. Right next to her couch, she had a framed portrait of Saint James the Great, sitting on his white horse, saber in hand, on the attack. She loved the image of this man. Brave. Courageous. Strong.*

*Faustin, Fanol and Ézéchiel's father, had fallen dead beside his mistress on his return from Miami. He was spent and had given all his savings to Cilianise, who knew how to wait him out. Then after his death, Aunt Cilianise no longer wanted a man of flesh and blood. While waiting for Faustin,* she had nourished her taste for absence. And Ogou had filled that void.

Aunt Cilianise had invested heavily in this union: her red dress was magnificent and the altar for Ogou was sumptuous with food, drinks, and bright red handkerchiefs surrounding machetes. The service dragged on because Ogou was playing with Aunt Cilianise's patience, and for three hours she did not move from her chair in front of the altar, beside an empty chair. Her patience was pure. Aunt Cilianise knew that god was a capricious lover. Then she waited. That would be her role. To wait. She had already discarded her mind, like too small a piece of clothing. She went, mad and naked, on a path known only to herself. I did not realize it until later. Too late. And at my expense.

Dieudonné was shaken several times by a slight tremor. Possession took him by surprise and he resisted each time by closing his eyes, hitting his forehead with his palm as if to wake up. To return to the surface of his own consciousness. He lost his footing, staggered, got back up with the help of Fanol, then of Yvnel, and held on. All around, the singing and drums had already begun the couplets to call the bridegroom. He demanded the bottle of clairin. He sat down and kindled the fire. His trembling grew so violent that Dieudonné was thrown down, legs and arms in the air. And then, in an entirely opposite movement, he stood upright like a palm tree, his eyes staring at the void. The songs rose in intensity:

> M'achté yon bèl manchèt pou Papa Ogou o
> Yon boutèy rhum pou Ogou Féray o
> Yon mouchwa rouj pou Papa Ogou o
> *I bought a beautiful machete for Ogou*
> *A bottle of rum for Ogou Féray*
> *A red scarf for papa Ogou*

*Ogou assumed the posture of the warrior marching, grand gestures with his arms. A young* hounsi *held out the sacred machete and tied his red handkerchief around his neck. He demanded a dry* clairin *and a cigar. Then he paced the room, whipping his machete around in all directions, warding off an invisible danger and dozens of opponents. And then, suddenly, he froze, remembering why he was there. Obviously he was looking for the bride. Someone in the crowd said to him: "Papa Ogou, your bride, she is here. Right there. Turn around."*

Ogou sé ou min m
Ki min nin m isit
Pran ka m, pran kam
*Ogou, it's you*
*Who brought me here*
*Be careful, be careful*

*Ogou joined Cilianise on the chair in front of the altar, and Julio, le Pè Savann, who had succeeded Érilien, was the formal officiator. Cilianise promised to receive him as a woman receives a lover and put a ring on her finger.*

*Aunt Cilianise's wedding reconciled Anse Bleue with its old dreams. Those of always. The dreams where the promises of fresh water from the streams poured into rivers which, with all their power, threw themselves into the sea as far as the afterlife.*

*Since then, Ogou has occupied the center of Aunt Cilianise's life. "Ogou gason solid oh," she liked to coo, touting his strength. Sometimes she smiled alone at the absent, her only companion, her friend, her lover.*

*The most faithful, the sweetest, the bravest. She smiled at this bust of fog which she preferred to any man's flesh. She no longer traded except for with the Mysterious, the Invisible, the Angel, the Saint. She waited for him some evenings, dressed for a ball, perfumed for bed. She was waiting for him in the violent happiness with which one receives a husband. Ogou left her after every reunion, his absence like a voluptuous blanket. Aunt Cilianise never knew how to talk about it. She said nothing. She laughed. Ogou had tied her tongue. Had taken possession of all her words of pleasure. Her past, present, and future words.*

*I wondered later if, to put it simply, if this wasn't cause for celebration. And I, Cétoute Olmène Thérèse, loved Aunt Cilianise's lust for an absent man a hundred times more present than all the others. Perhaps it was because no one as perfect as Jimmy had come to her that she had chosen Ogou. The first time I saw Jimmy, I thought that.*

*Mother and Altagrâce shunned all the services and had chosen the narrow door of virtue with the charismatic sisters, blistering their fingers and kneeling on the steps of the churches. Me, I was tearing myself up in wanting Jimmy. I played at pretending to push him away with as much vehemence as he sought me. His gaze palpated me like I was a ripe fruit. I subjected him to a Lenten fast. A long Good Friday. Dry bread and water. Which of us is the prey? And the hunter? I don't know. I try a game that I do not know. A game that enchants me. Sitting at the entrance to the Blue Moon, Jimmy looks at the world with his eyes half closed, his chair turned backward. And it always starts with a downpour in a dust storm.*

*Maybe Jimmy just gave me some leftovers that I ate from his hand. Jimmy threw me crumbs. He made me play with fire. I spent days and nights yearning for the look of an indifferent man. Why, at some point in our lives, do we feel this need to play with fire?*

*To sully our reason with madness? Why is that? I played with fire. I sullied my reason with madness, too. In my own way.*

*With my right eye I see the sea. I take my time when I look at her. Especially since the four men have stopped in their tracks. Despite the morning breeze, they sweat. Wipe their foreheads. The squat one takes off his red cardigan. I hope a stray dog does not come to put his wet muzzle right against my face. To sniff me.*

*The night of the hurricane, nobody dared to look out to the sea. No one. They would have been too scared. A whole village walking in fear and rain. Even when the sun started to rise timidly, they preferred to look at the side of the hills overlooking Anse Bleue. Nobody except Abner. Abner is the bravest of us all. In any case, they did not see me leave, nor the sea close in on me like the lid of a tomb.*

37.

When he was old enough, Abner also wanted to draw us toward a world that did not exist. A world that had been dangled before his eyes by the new sellers of miracles. A world whose contours he began to outline in his head. Abner only has the word development in his mouth. Development here. Development over there. "If you cut the trees, no development. If you plant the beans in the coffee fields, the land will disappear, no development. If you defecate in rivers, no development." We planted the beans in the coffee fields all the way up, cut down the trees and defecated in the waters. He believed that the arrival of the prophet, leader of the party of the Destitute in power, would change everything and us with it.

Abner's anger was equal to his disappointment. But one day he stopped staring at the world with bitterness. We did not know where he had gotten the courage, but he had found it. He dug a well, tested out seeds, and organized a cooperative. A whole production that his brother Éliphète did not believe in. Éliphète did not believe in much. With Abner, there were explanations, more explanations, always explanations, to describe this world that would finally be developed, wild with happiness.

Jean-Paul, a descendant of the Mésidors, and François, one of Madame Frétillon nephews, had come to be the head of a team that was to embark on an ambitious program for irrigation and the establishment of the cooperative. They had arrived with the same sandals that the men and women of the party of the Destitute had, and the same straw hats. Jean-Paul walked barefoot sometimes, just to give his soft and smooth soles a chance to be hurt. François asked questions about what we ate, how we organized our families, what our cultivation methods were. The other one never stopped surveying the five villages to plan the cooperative. Or he walked around the plains and hills to understand where the water could come from and whether it was still possible to find much depth. There were meetings, rallies in the area and sometimes in Port-au-Prince. Abner returned more transformed every time. He had really felt like a leader when, after a meeting where he had spoken, he was invited to the residence of Jean-Paul Laboule. There he drank whiskey, a rum for the rich, and listened to music as sweet as the murmur of a woman.

The years passed, resembling each other. Between the drawings of the lottery, every day, Dieudonné told us what he learned from the radios. The prophet had transformed the hunger-stricken, poor, and cursed like us, into organized gangs armed to the tooth—you didn't want to run into them. White people came to see them, they took them for Western heroes, warriors, and were fond of their names of the night: Jojo-mort-aux-rats, Hervé-piment-piké, or Chuck Norris. Names that sent chills up your spine. Names suggesting that these men could make you their next meal. But these white people loved sensationalism. So they wrote articles for the newspapers and filmed them to frighten other whites who would be watching them on television. We also saw them on televisions in Baudelet, between soccer matches. For a few seconds we told ourselves that it was still good to live in Anse Bleue, Roseaux, or even Baudelet. And not in Port-au-Prince.

One day when Fanol had visited Anse Bleue, he and Abner got into a bad fight. Fanol defended his meaningless job and denied that what remained of the meager cake was shared openly with everyone. That the appetite of all had been whetted, but that the cream and three quarters of the cake had been carried off along the way. That people would also disappear forever. That others died, riddled with bullets by strangers. Always unknown. That some of those who disappeared reappeared because their parents had paid. Fanol denied everything. Oxéna and Yvnel encouraged him to deny so he wouldn't get into trouble.

But they also spoke in a hushed tones about a new miraculous manna. White as the flour of the loaves when Jesus fed the five thousand. Planes landed at night to deliver this manna. Or let it fall from heaven in bundles. Entire lands had been cleared for this single harvest.

In the truck rented from a man in Roseaux, Éliphète had seen much of the country and heard a slew of words between Anse

Bleue, Roseaux, Baudelet, and Port-au-Prince. He had claimed one day, in a moment of inspiration, that the miracles would not take place. "The only miracle will come from heaven and it will be poisoned. Because it is the devil who will send it on metal wings. The metal wings will cross the sky. And this manna, they'll eat it sitting on stones of fire, under a dry sky, among the last cacti and *bayahondes*, between the discotheques, the glimmering 4x4s, the gangsters, the tramps from the lounges and the AK47s." He had moved his arms in a way to say that these were weapons used to kill. Éliphète had been right.

"The world is a difficult place. You cheat and trick and lie, or you die," he concluded. "I don't want to die," cried Cétoute. She was barely twelve years old. We did not know where this cry came from. He had taken her by surprise. And we all laughed. And then Cétoute went to join her mother and the charismatic sisters on the narrow porch in front of her house. She repeated three Hail Marys with them to forget for a moment the tremendous and terrible surprises that life had in store at this time, in this place.

38.

On one morning in April, a new 4x4 was swallowing up kilometer after kilometer, making passersby since Port-au-Prince turn around. In the villages, our eyes caught it like claws. When the 4x4 reached what seemed like the top of the world, Anse Bleue offered all of itself to Jimmy's eyes. The sea was a shining plate as far as the eye could see, put there to send back all the power of the sun, as if the condemned land was caught between two destinies, to burn or to be swallowed up. He scanned these hamlets like little blisters on the sand. Putrid. Nauseating. The driver started a long diatribe about this earth which, shamelessly, showed its guts and scars. Abandoned by all. Jimmy was deaf and indifferent to the whining and boring drone of the driver, whom he asked after a moment to be quiet because it was hot. Jimmy wanted to be alone with his thoughts. Without the crutches of a man whose opinion did not matter. The disorder was even greater than he had imagined and it didn't upset him. Not at all. Disorder was his element, his breath, his water and his sky. He rubbed his hands together, a broad smile on his lips. To the astonishment of the driver, who had seen the surrender of the man with a black hat and thick glasses and the blue uniforms, the rise of the party of the Destitute with its prophet, its bearers of good news, becoming after a few years richer than those of the party of the Rich, who had sharpened the same machetes and crackled the uzis.

The driver wondered what might make his passenger smile: "Mr. Jimmy, it's like in the Bible, it has become difficult today to separate the wheat from the chaff."

"I leave that work to God," retorted Jimmy. At this, the driver resolved to speak of the rain and the good weather, and not to mention the high cost of living, let alone the desolation of the countryside. He was not going to preach or make enemies and handed over the what little remained of his soul to God every Sunday and every Tuesday fasting at the renovated church of the Pentecostalists.

"How are the authorities in the area?"

The driver spat out, almost with emphasis:

"Very serious people."

And after repeating the "very serious" three times, he praised the qualities of each of the commissioners, the mayor and his assessors, the deputies, and the senator. Jimmy did not believe a word and in his head said to himself: "He's lying to me, but this lousy bunch doesn't deserve any better." He was eager to reach Morin Hill after Baudelet. "It is not possible, Baudelet, where are you? Perhaps, feeling my arrival, you went back underground?" With this thought, he laughed out loud. And his eyes shone with the mad glare of those men for whom hell is the preferred state of mind.

Jimmy murmured something between his teeth that the driver couldn't hear. When the latter asked him to repeat what he had just said, he replied that it was nothing important, just the ramblings of a man gripped by emotion. The driver did not believe a word and, of course, did not insist.

The driver had trouble going along this rocky road. The new jeep, a yellow SUV, made a spectacle among pedestrians and motorists, peasants along the road.

When they finally reached the market in Roseaux, Jimmy whispered: "I am back and you will feel it. A Mésidor is back and that's something." This time he had uttered his words so loudly that the driver could hear him and swallowed his own spit. Jimmy was a member of the Rich, but he had his ins with the party of the Destitute and was preparing, with his accomplices on both sides, to lend a hand to the disorder.

He had to do it quickly, very quickly. His grandfather, Tertulien Mésidor, was in agony and he, the son of Mérien Mésidor, disowned a few years earlier, wanted to be accepted by this grandfather whom he did not know. To be accepted in order to redeem his father. But also to take, to seize. Tertulien, pursued because of his quarrels with the men in blue, had taken refuge in the Dominican Republic and later had returned in secret. Waiting for the tide to turn. In a country where the most dependable weapon is erasure; the most lucrative defense, evasion. To let the storm pass, before spreading our wings again and running with the pack of the moment.

The driver of the yellow SUV recounted, the following Sunday, in the square of the Pentecostal church in Roseaux, Jimmy's arrival, and, at the market in Baudelet, Tertulien's servants told us the story of the last conversation between the dying man and his grandson. By way of receiving them in as far out as our part of the countryside, we knew that the pack of the moment, with or without uniforms of the armies of the world, were coming from every corner to hunt or cut up this corpse that had become too cumbersome. Haiti, *yon chaj twò lou,* a thorn in the foot of America.

We, in Anse Bleue and in the other villages, were like a wayward horse, which could not be coaxed by cunning nor by force. So we were fenced in, in an enclosure. And we are still humming inside ourselves:

> *Chèn ki chèn, nou krazé li*
> *Ki diré pou kòd o*
> We were able to break the chains
> But what about these thin ropes?

39.

When Tertulien saw this grandson, who had come from so far away, he still couldn't keep stop the memory of Mérien from rising to the surface and spoiling his joy.

Marie-Elda, Tertulien Mésidor's wife, was made of a fragility that contrasted with her husband's unremitting rage. No servant remembered hearing her say one word too many, one word too loud, one word awry. Marie-Elda Mesidor seemed to look out at the other side of life without paying attention to what was happening here, in plain sight. Under her nose. We were never explained her presence in such a place, her presence on a sheet next too such a man.

If each new birth had left her more frail than the previous one, that had not stopped her, without a tear or a cry, from pushing ten children into the world at the pleasure of her husband: Osias, Boileau, Pamphile, Candelon, Théophile, Joséphine, Horace, Hermit, Madrine, and Mérien. All of them, like Marie-Elda, obeyed their father's every word. All except Mérien, the youngest, who had come into the world with a poisonous stinging in his chest. Like all gifted souls, the tiger's cub began to resemble its parent very early on.

The last time Tertulien had beaten Mérien, everyone had thought he was going to kill him. With a blackjack as a whip, he had lacerated his skin, then bashed, bashed his bare hands into his chest, face, arms. Like he wanted to exorcise some evil spirit from his son. Mérien bore the blows until the moment a rage from the bottom of his guts made him leap, head forward like a young bull, and fight back with all his might. Tertulian Mésidor fell backward. Son nailed father to the ground, placing his hands around his neck, ready to tighten, hard, on his Adam's apple. If it weren't for the cries of his mother, the interference of Osias, the eldest of the brothers, and the cries of the servants, perhaps Mérien would have committed the irreparable. Tertulien, standing up, seized a machete and threatened Mérien, who retreated, looking at his father in the eyes. None of the other brothers could catch him. He ran off and behind his back he heard Tertulien, his father, cursing him for five generations. Mérien Mésidor, a few days later, we learned from the most talkative servants, joined one of his aunts in America. That was many years ago.

Tertulien was moved. Which loosened the hand of that pain that painted horrible grimaces on his face. His mouth seemed to want to snatch all the air around him. An inaudible murmur came from the bottom of his throat. He only had the strength to stroke the hand of his grandson, to put a hand on his hair and to hand him a paper. He asked him to write down the names of the men and women on whom he could rely. For anything. For everything. "Take note, my son!"

Tertulien Mésidor, in a final outburst, sat up in his bed and gathered his last strength to cast words out of his mouth like a flamethrower:

"My son, I have no remorse and I will not beg for God's mercy. By way of compromises and dirty deeds, I accumulated a small fortune, property, property, and more property. I am wealthier than the residents of these five villages combined. Nothing ever stopped me when I wanted to kill, steal, rape. Nothing. It was very nice those days when I had blood on my hands. It's like God cleared a path for me every time I moved forward."

He stopped to laugh out loud, his eyes shining with dementia.

"I saw everything on this island. Until the second occupation by the Marines. I say second occupation, my son, because there will be others. And I always got the same respect from everyone, do you hear me?"

Jimmy nodded, "Yes, yes."

And Tertulien clung to his shirt:

"Yes, respect for gold and power. Nothing else, my grandson, nothing else."

Before dying, Tertulien wanted to have the pleasure of recounting his crimes. He uttered his last words, falling back on his bed. He died with his eyes wide open.

The news of Jimmy's return spread along the paths, from one hut to another, in the aisles of the markets. From one garden to the next. Then it seemed to us once again that nothing had happened. That the party of the Destitute had not existed. Some of us began to distrust their memories. Going so far as to believe that our fevers were only the fruit of a collective hallucination. That the misery from before, from under the man with black hat and thick glasses, was perhaps better than the one that had planted its fangs in our lives today.

Jimmy decided to take it all back, even more than he'd came back for. He would be a curse. Him too.

"I'm back and you're going to feel it."

40.

*It's Jimmy who killed me. And it all started with the plane. It was a Friday and I had left Baudelet like I did every Friday to return to Anse Bleue.*

It's true that the first time the plane flew over Anse Bleue, in the middle of the night, we were awoken with a start. And my father, still asleep, called us one after the other in a low voice, with words that fear distorted, like there was a piece of potato, still burning hot, in his mouth. He called us to ask if we heard this strange noise over our heads. Drowsy, with eyes half closed, we too heard the rumbling that had just punched a big hole in the night. We first believed it was a sign from heaven or from the land under the waters.

After three turns above Anse Bleue, the noise of the plane faded, as if silence swallowed it as the plane went toward the Lavandou Morne. After a moment that felt like an eternity, we heard nothing more.

Woken up much earlier than usual, my father, Aunt Cilianise, Yvnel, the children, all spoke quietly in front of their huts. The children ran between our legs and mingled their hollering with the crowing of the rooster, the barking of the dog that kept going in different directions. We spoke in sentences that said and did not say. A real game of hide and seek with ourselves. The seconds were full of words and yet cluttered with silence. But we understood each other, as we always did, when a silent word like a dark presence came to take its place between us. All this unrest was returning us to a great tumult. So sometimes we looked at the sea, sometimes to the sky swaddled in blue and pink on the slope of the hills. And I, Cétoute Florival, I heard time gnaw at us like an army of rats.

Altagrâce pointed to what had been the trajectory of the plane just above our hut, before Uncle Yvnel interrupted by proposing an unbeatable argument that seemed to be authoritative: he knew how a plane was made, because Léosthène had described it to him in great detail—the airplane seats, the belt tied around the waist, the turbulence that turns your stomach, the hostesses who fill in the forms for this cohort of illiterates that we are, that daily forces the gates of America.

*Abner avoided the question of the trajectory, which had already caused too much drooling, but assumed that sullen and skeptical gaze that knew enough to be worried and not enough to share this worry with us. For a few days, he twirled his beard and settled on, "I do not like this plane. I do not like what it's going to bring us."When asked what he meant by these words, he just concluded that, in his opinion, the aircraft had landed on the Mésidors's property.*

*Abner ranked the event in the long list of those which had upended the quiet life of Anse Bleue in recent months, after having disturbed that of the whole island. Cilianise went on, speaking from a jaw swollen by words that were too heavy.*

*Oxéna was about to give her opinion, when Dieudonné, my father, gave her a gesture to be silent. Then, looking up at the sky four times in a row, he spoke in a voice that meant that the debate was once and for all over. Then, without having to mention it, it was as clear to Dieudonné as it was to all of us that we would swear to all those who were not from Anse Bleue that we had seen nothing, heard nothing that night.*

*Pulling up the collar of his torn sweater, he concluded that it had been too long since the Spirits had been fed, and that all these events were there to remind us.*

*I turn around and go back. One last time. Approaching my second death. The real one.*

*"You seek me, you will find me." Why does this phrase haunt me?*

*The second time I meet Jimmy, I'm already a fool for love.*

*I forgot many things I wanted to remember and remember things I should forget. But that's how it goes. My soul, my* bon ange, *do not abandon me. I ramble, I ramble…*

*I haunted the village for three nights. Crawling between the interstices. Without flesh and bones. Flesh and bones already dissolved by salt and water. Splitting the shadows like the bow of a boat.*

*I did not want to leave Anse Bleue. Not like that. Fortunately, as often happens, the direction of the wind suddenly changed in the night: I did not go to the high seas, but I turned back. I walked along the coast. It was like Loko, Agwé, Aïda, Wêdo and all the others did not want me to leave Anse Bleue and its surroundings. Not so early, not so quickly…*

*So, all night, I haunted the village. Until the early morning. My strong scent, like a marine animal, penetrated everywhere without making anyone retch. I snuck in between the walls of the huts of the village, lifted the few frayed curtains of the rickety windows, blew open the poorly built doors like a headwind, and howled their names, but nobody seemed to see me. Nobody seemed to hear me. No one. They only said my name in muffled sobs.*

*The procession stopped and the four men set me on the sand. This is their second break. They are thirsty and ask for water from two women who left work in the early morning to come to join the small crowd accompanying me.*

*This morning the world is beautiful, the sky will soon be washed after the rains. I think of Abner, who never lets himself be prey to misfortune. Who always refuses to follow its black corridors. While I, long drawn by the void, I sink into Olmène's steps.*

41.

*Altagrâce swore to have seen Jimmy on the road between Ti Pistache and Roseaux in the pickup that Octavius, a man from Roseaux, described. He's also the one who told the story.*

As soon as they had fallen asleep, he, who was a light sleeper, perceived a stir, murmuring outside. Looking through a hole in the window, Octavius distinctly saw the contours of a big new green pickup. "Two men came down," he claimed. "I recognized the short, bulky man who spoke only Spanish, he had a bottle in his hand. The other man, probably the one who was driving," Octavius went on, "lit a lighter. They know how to do it, I tell you. Specialists. And I saw the flame approaching the rag. I shuddered in thinking, 'There's no way they're going to do that,' and I shouted. And I woke up my brother Brignol. I woke up my mother. The squat man's arm relaxed and the flame made the arc of a circle coming straight at us. The bottle hit the wood on the window and I pulled back. The blast nearly burst our eardrums. The flames ran on the floor, crackling, crackling, the crackling took over everything, everywhere. We ran out to escape the fire and the suffocating smell of gasoline. And we all heard the driver throw out the words: 'Next time, we kill you, Octavius. It's a warning.' I had to keep myself from wetting my pants. Because these men are terrible."

Then, very quietly, he told Altagrâce how, two days later, Jimmy had threatened him even more seriously: "Next time I will debase you, massisi,★ before killing you." He had said it leaning against his car, a toothpick between his lips. I wanted to ask Altagrâce to keep quiet. Stop spreading gossip. But I did not say anything. I didn't say anything to Cocotte or Yveline either

"Where did you meet the squat man?" "How did you know Jimmy?" Octavius had become entangled in confused explanations. In fact, Octavius had been working for Jimmy. For his mother, for the neighbors, for everybody. But no one had believed him. The next day, I met Octavius and I hated him, that snitch…

"You're jealous, come on!" I repeated to myself, silently, several times in row.

So when the plane flew over Anse Bleue a second time, we had already been warned. Éliphète had seen it right. Even more than Abner. I wanted to know more. So I went hunting. On the hunt for a vandal of a man.

The next day, I surprised Jimmy, not far from the Blue Moon, handing a package to Octavius. Jimmy saw me and ran after me to catch up. When I turned around, I did not say anything. I would have been too frightened to betray myself by explaining everything. I preferred to thicken the layers of silence that encloses everything in the tomb of forgetting. I gave into sleep as one abandons herself to death. Wasn't I born in a shameless time?

Despite the recommendations and warnings of the teacher, radio, and CASEC* members who came to warn us that a major hurricane was going to hit the coast, I took my sweet time. Who knows why.

There are those big mounds of salt and foam on the sand.

But in this twilight three days ago, I saw nothing. Nothing. Too busy trying to breathe. Too busy trying not to see everything coming next.

"Do not do what you might regret," my mother hammers. "Don't do it."

Later, the wind blew without stopping. Ripping branches from trees. Stirring up the leaves in gusts. I thought of Pastor Fortuné's sermons, which Ézéchiel and Oxéna related at Pentacostalist church. Noah's Ark. And I imagined that the sea had taken the place of the sky and poured all of its water on us. I really believed that. And that soon men, women, animals, and children...

Bursts of water from the black sky spilled over Anse Bleue and the purple sea. The wind, in all this water, unleashed itself, deepening the swirls of air and rain, making giant waves on the rocks, uprooting the trees, ripping off sheet metal, undoing thatched roofs.

Very quickly, lightning slashed the sky like an old calabash. I pretended to listen to the advice. To return. Instead I hid behind the bayahondes at the top of the dunes.

*I fall and lose my footing. I no longer spit out water in sonorous gurgles on the surface of the water. My heart abruptly stops its free run.*

*Loko, in the voice of the wind, blew the whole afternoon until I staggered, until I fell on my knees. It is one of those hurricanes with the wind that enchants and drives you mad. It rose into a crash banging against my temples. Suddenly, a pure joy assailed me. I remember a kind of drunkenness taking hold of me. I was free, in the wind. In the sea. Given to the big wild heart. Crossing the same violent eddies. I wanted to cry out: "My love, where are you? Do not be afraid. It is only the fascination of the moon. That's all, my love."*

*And then, above my head and against my neck, two hands that force me to sink into the waves. Despite myself. Despite the breath that begins to leave me, I grab in every direction. My gestures are as abrupt as they are desperate. I struggle with all the strength of my arms, with all the strength of my legs. I struggle to the point of exhaustion. Until breath abandons me.*

*But now I'm losing my footing. I drink the water until I suffocate. I collapse like an animal who is knocked down. Between my thighs, a hand, a flesh that tears me. I turn around. My astonished eyes roll up. And suddenly, the liquid darkness. Colder and colder. In that night of wind and water, he grabbed me by the shoulders and held my head under water before rushing into the bayahondes.*

*Approaching Anse Bleue, despite their great fatigue, the four men walked faster. I perceive, in the distance, our hut and all the others, still wrapped in the fog of the fable. All faces turned north. In the direction of the advancing cortege. Men sweat in large beads. Their arms, though robust, tremble. A dead woman, that weighs a lot.*

*I hear a sort of uncontrollable sound, like something that would come from the gut of an animal being slaughtered. And which, after having dug itself out of the black hole in the deepest bones within the flesh, climbs into the chest, squeezes the throat, and spurts out of the mouth into the fresh air. My mother shouts my name very clearly in a deafening treble: "Cétouuuuuute, Cétouuuuuute."*

*Anse Bleue cries, but soon Anse Bleue will do everything to keep me from roaming around. So that everyone can very quickly think of me without being sucked into the other side. I will come back only to do them good. There is the side of grief that still belongs to life, and there are the gates of death.*

42.

The sun had already unraveled the last shreds of clouds when Abner saw a strange procession from Pointe Sable arrive on the north side of the beach in Anse Bleue. The cry of his mother Philomène tore the air, made tatters of the sky…Dieudonné, bellowing out his grief, held himself together as best he could. Abner felt quite alone. Alone. Desperate. He waited a moment and swallowed reluctantly. His lips began to quiver, and his vision blurred. He felt a need to cry and struggled against this desire by rubbing his eyes quickly in the crook of his elbow. He went to join the procession. We saw him leave and followed. He took out his cell phone and dialed the number of the police station in Roseaux. For the first time, men of order and justice would tread the land of Anse Bleue.

After having spoken to them, he told us that he had regained the courage that he thought had abandoned him forever. He thought of the harvest that would be more generous this year because of the irrigation works of Jean-Paul and François, because of the construction of the Pentecostal clinic that was done, because of the cooperative. All this put a little mercy in his heart. For a few seconds. Just a few seconds. He did not give up…He went on. He almost staggered.

Then, we followed Abner, so at ease in the *bayahondes* that blurred the path ahead. The way to tomorrow. These thickets where we could see no way out. Unlike us, Abner, with an invisible machete, seemed to be tearing out bushes and going on. We measure our steps by his.

43.

*My real death will begin when they wash me, cut my fingernails and a few strands of hair, which will be carefully preserved in a vial. And Dieudonné, my father, Cilianise, Fanol and all the others will entrust me with messages for those I will see or see again before they will. Dieudonné will murmur the three sacred passages into my ears. I will go alone under the waters, leaving my protective gods in the water of the calabash right next to me.*

*When, after forty days, they take me out of the water, I shall at last turn my eyes toward the light, and it will be, for my people, the beginning of a companionship with them. My death will no longer be a torment. I will bandage the wounds. I will sweeten the bitterness. I will intercede with the lwas, the Invisibles.*

*I would ask Altagrâce and my mother, if I could, to put me in my white dress, like Erica's in* All My Children, *and put on my red, high-heeled sandals. Altagrâce, my sister, knows exactly where they are, in a trunk beneath my bed.*

*I would like to arrive in Guinée, to be with the Grand Maître, wearing the dress of a queen and with feet on fire. That's how I'm prepared. I am Fréda's daughter.*

# GENEALOGICAL TREE

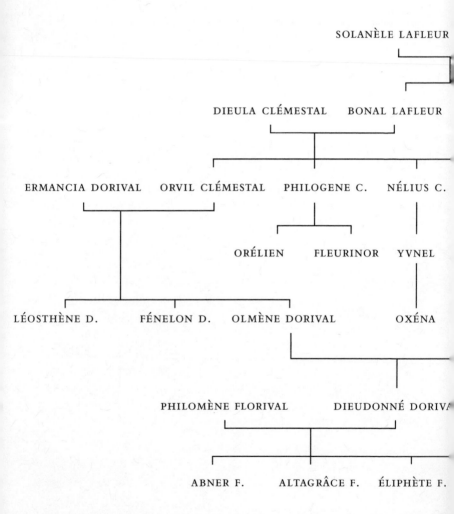

SOLANÈLE LAFLEUR

DIEULA CLÉMESTAL    BONAL LAFLEUR

ERMANCIA DORIVAL    ORVIL CLÉMESTAL    PHILOGENE C.    NÉLIUS C.

ORÉLIEN    FLEURINOR    YVNEL

LÉOSTHÈNE D.    FÉNELON D.    OLMÈNE DORIVAL    OXÉNA

PHILOMÈNE FLORIVAL    DIEUDONNÉ DORIVA

ABNER F.    ALTAGRÂCE F.    ÉLIPHÈTE F.

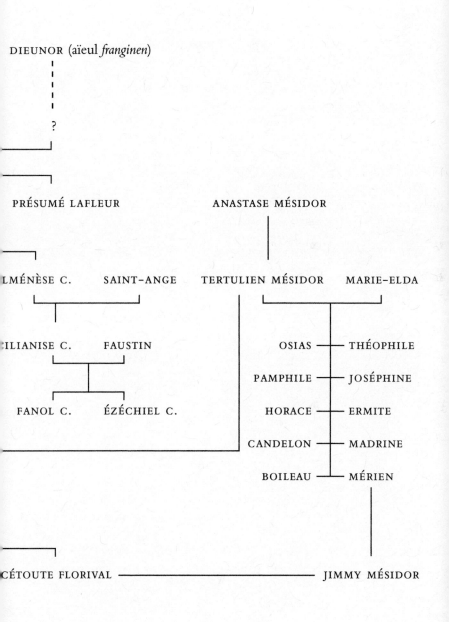

DIEUNOR (aïeul *franginen*)

?

PRÉSUMÉ LAFLEUR    ANASTASE MÉSIDOR

:LMÉNÈSE C.  SAINT-ANGE  TERTULIEN MÉSIDOR  MARIE-ELDA

:ILIANISE C.  FAUSTIN    OSIAS ——— THÉOPHILE

            PAMPHILE ——— JOSÉPHINE

FANOL C.  ÉZÉCHIEL C.    HORACE ——— ERMITE

           CANDELON ——— MADRINE

           BOILEAU ——— MÉRIEN

CÉTOUTE FLORIVAL ————————————— JIMMY MÉSIDOR

# GLOSSARY

*The spelling of the Creole was simplified by the author to render it more accessible to the French reader. All notes are the author's unless otherwise noted.*

*Agwé*  The divinity of the sea, of oceans.

*Ancêtres marrons*  Escaped African slaves (trans.).

*Arbre véritable*  The breadfruit tree.

*Asson*  A hollow calabash filled with small bones, a sort of rattle, which serves as a ritual scepter to the officiator during voodoo ceremonies.

*Badji*  The sanctuary of the voodoo temple.

*Baka*  An evil creature.

*Bain de chance*  A bath specially prepared to attract the favors of the divinities.

*Banane pesée*  Fried plantains.

*Bâton gaïac*  A stick of guaiac wood, particularly solid.

*Batouelle*  A bottle.

*Bayahonde*  A wild shrub.

*Bois-fouillé*  A boat built in the trunk of a tree.

*Borlette*  The lottery.

*Bougie baleine*  A simple candle, originally made with whale fat.

*Cacos*  Rebels who resisted the American occupation of Haiti (trans.).

*Candélabre*  A variety of plants used to build fences in the countryside.

*Carabella*  A fabric made of coarse cotton.

*Carreaux*  A traditional Haitian unit for measuring land, corresponding to about 3.19 acres.

*Casec*  The French acronym for conseil d'administration de section communale, or Boards of Directors of Communal Sections.

*Chanson-pointe*  A song that obliquely comments on an event that took place in a community or a politi-cal issue.

*Cher maître, chère maîtresse*  A master who owns property and isn't accountable to anyone but himself.

*Choukèt larouzé*  The deputy head of a section who, before 1986, ensured order and security in the countryside.

*Chrétien-vivant*   A human being.

*Clairin*   A distilled spirit made from sugar cane.

*Coucouye*   A firefly.

*Coumbite*   A form of collective work, mutual assistance.

*Damballa*   The serpent divinity who is often depicted alongside his wife Aida Wèdo.

*Danti*   The head of a lakou, who wields great decision-making power.

*Démembré*   A piece of family land where the spiritual attributes of a lineage reside.

*Désounin*   The ceremony that takes place after death to prepare passage to the after life. The word can also be used as an adjective meaning "disconcerted."

*Djon-djon*   A black mushroom that colors rice or meat and gives them a particular taste.

*Doko*   A remote and clandestine place that served as a refuge for insurgents after independence.

*Don*   A powerful landowner.

*Drapeau*   A flag made of bright, glittering colors and symbolizing the protective divinities of the lakou.

*Erzuli Dantò*   Another counterpart to Erzuli, who symbolizes endurance and strength.

*Erzuli Fréda*   The divinity of love, beautiful, coquettish, sensual and lavish; one of the three most im-portant female divinities.

*Femme-jardin*   A common law wife charged with cultivating a parcel of land for a master.

*Franginen*   An individual born in Africa who survived the revolution of 1804.

*Gaguère*   A highly prized space reserved for cockfighting.

*Gédé*   The divinity who symbolizes life and death.

*Gourde*   Haitian currency.

*Gran Bwa*   The divinity of trees and forests.

*Grand Maître*   The name of God in the voodoo religion.

*Griot*   Fried pork.

*Grouillades*   Swaying hips.

*Guayabelle*   The typical shirt of the Caribbean (guayabera).

*Guildive*  A small distillery.

*Guinée*  In voodoo, after a person dies, his or her soul returns to freedom in Africa, in Guinea (trans.).

Habitation  A large property.

*Hougan*  A voodoo prayer.

*Hounsi*  An initiate into voodoo.

*Jardin*  A field or a property belonging to a farmer.

*Jeunesse*  Woman of ill-repute, prostitute.


*Kabich*  Unleavened bread.

*Kamoken*  Opponents to the Duvaliers, father and son, from 1957 to 1986.

*Kanzo*  A voodoo initiation rite that protects a person from being burned by fire.

*Kasav*  A cake made of cassava flour.


*Labalenn*  The Haitian divinity of water.

*Lakou*  The dwellings of an extended family.

*Lalo*  Wild spinach.

*Lambi*  A conch used as a horn by peasants.

*Lampe bobèche*  A receptacle where a wick is dipped in oil.

*Lasirenn*  The divinity who pulls the dead under water to take them to Africa.

*Legba*  A divinity who opens the way and is invoked at the beginning of religious services to open the way to other divinities.

*Loko*  The divinity of the wind.

*Lwa*  A divinity in the voodoo religion.


*Majò jon*  Someone who, in the rara carnival (see below), juggles a stick or a cross made of four branch-es of equal length.

*Mambo*  A voodoo priestess.

*Mantègue*  Lard.

*Mapou*  A sacred tree with big trunk and deep roots, with the same function as the baobab tree in Africa.

*Massisi*  A homosexual.

*Matelote*  A mistress.

*Mèt tèt*  The divinity most important to a person.


*Nordé*  The wind of north.

*Ogou*   The divinity of war and fire, whose Catholic double is Saint James the Great.

*Paille*   A name for marijuana.

*Paquet wanga*   A bundle filled with ingredients containing magical powers.

*Pétro*   A Créole divinity, not of African origin, deemed violent.

*Plaçage*   The most common type of marital relationship, a form of concubinage.

*Point*   The power given to somebody by a hougan or a mambo.

*Poto-mitan*   The central pillar to a voodoo colonnade, through which the divinities descend.

*Priyé deyò*   All of the prayers which precede a religious service.

*Ralé min nin vini*   A magic powder used to attract somebody.

*Rangé*   Intended to do harm.

*Rapadou*   Brown sugar.

*Rara*   A carnival in the countryside that starts after Ash Wednesday.

*Rigoise*   A whip made from a blackjack.

*Roi*   Somebody who presides over the family clan and is generally the leader of the lakou.

*Simbi*   One of the divinities of the sea.

*Son*   A cuban dance from the beginning of the twentieth century.

*Tambour assòtòr*   The largest of the drums.

*Tap-tap*   Shared taxi or bus.

*Tchaka*   Very rich dishes prepared with millet, beans and other vegetables.

*Trempé*   A distilled liquor steeped with herbs and spices.

*Vaccine*   A wind instrument made from bamboo.

*Vèvè*   A drawing depicting a divinity.

*Zaka*   The divinity of the earth, the gardens, and the peasants.

YANICK LAHENS, considered one of Haiti's most prominent authors, was born in Port-au-Prince. She moved to France where she attended university before returning to Haiti to teach literature at the Ecole Normale Supérieure (ENS) and Université d'Etat d'Haïti (UEH), in addition to working at the Haitian Ministry of Culture. In 1998 she became the executive director of UNESCO's National Committee for "Route de l'Esclavage" ("Road to Slavery"), a project focused on the effects of slavery in Haitian society. She is currently an editor with Editions Henri Deschamps, a board member on the Conseil International d'Etudes Francophones (International Council of Francophone Studies), and is a founding member of the Haitian Writers Union. Known for her vivid portrayals of life in Haiti, Lahens is the author of a collection of critical essays and articles for Caribbean publications, including *Chemins critiques*, *Cultura*, and *Boutures*. She has published three collections of short stories and several award-winning novels. She was awarded the 2014 Prix Femina for *Moonbath*, and that same year was named Officier des Arts et des Lettres by the French Embassy in Haiti in recognition for her work in promoting French culture and literature throughout the world.

EMILY GOGOLAK is a journalist and translator from the French. She studied French Philosophy and Literature at the Université de la Sorbonne in Paris and is a graduate of Brown University in Comparative Literature. A former editorial staffer at *The New Yorker* and a James Reston Reporting Fellow at the *New York Times*, she now lives in Texas. Her writing focuses on migration, gender, and the US-Mexico border, and has appeared in *The New Yorker* online, the *New York Times*, *The Nation*, and *The Village Voice*, and in the anthology *City by City: Dispatches from the American Metropolis* (Farrar, Straus & Giroux, 2015). Her translations have been published in *The Brooklyn Rail*, *Lana Turner Journal of Poetry and Opinion*, and *The Review of Contemporary Fiction*. She won a 2015 French Voices Award for her translation of Yanick Lahens' *Moonbath*.

Thank you all
for your support.
We do this for you,
and could not do
it without you.

DEEP
VELLUM

## DEAR READERS,

Deep Vellum Publishing is a 501c3 nonprofit literary arts organization founded in 2013 with a threefold mission: to publish international literature in English translation; to foster the art and craft of translation; and to build a more vibrant book culture in Dallas and beyond. We are dedicated to broadening cultural connections across the English-reading world by connecting readers, in new and creative ways, with the work of international authors. We strive for diversity in publishing authors from various languages, viewpoints, genders, sexual orientations, countries, continents, and literary styles, whose works provide lasting cultural value and build bridges with foreign cultures while expanding our understanding of how the world thinks, feels, and experiences the human condition.

Operating as a nonprofit means that we rely on the generosity of tax-deductible donations from individual donors, cultural organizations, government institutions, and foundations. Your donations provide the basis of our operational budget as we seek out and publish exciting literary works from around the globe and build a vibrant and active literary arts community both locally and within the global society. Deep Vellum offers multiple donor levels, including LIGA DE ORO (\$5,000+) and LIGA DEL SIGLO (\$1,000+). Donors at various levels receive personalized benefits for their donations, including books and Deep Vellum merchandise, invitations to special events, and recognition in each book and on our website.

In addition to donations, we rely on subscriptions from readers like you to provide an invaluable ongoing investment in Deep Vellum that demonstrates a commitment to our editorial vision and mission. Subscribers are the bedrock of our support as we grow the readership for these amazing works of literature from every corner of the world. The investment our subscribers make allows us to demonstrate to potential donors and bookstores alike the support and demand for Deep Vellum's literature across a broad readership and gives us the ability to grow our mission in ever-new, ever-innovative ways.

In partnership with our sister company and bookstore, Deep Vellum Books, located in the historic cultural district of Deep Ellum in central Dallas, we organize and host literary programming such as author readings, translator workshops, creative writing classes, spoken word performances, and interdisciplinary arts events for writers, translators, and artists from across the globe. Our goal is to enrich and connect the world through the power of the written and spoken word, and we have been recognized for our efforts by being named one of the "Five Small Presses Changing the Face of the Industry" by *Flavorwire* and honored as Dallas's Best Publisher by *D Magazine*.

If you would like to get involved with Deep Vellum as a donor, subscriber, or volunteer, please contact us at deepvellum.org. We would love to hear from you.

Thank you all. Enjoy reading.
Will Evans, Founder & Publisher, Deep Vellum Publishing

## LIGA DE ORO ($5,000+)

Anonymous (2)

## LIGA DEL SIGLO ($1,000+)

Allred Capital Management

Ben & Sharon Fountain

David Tomlinson & Kathryn Berry

Judy Pollock

Life in Deep Ellum

Loretta Siciliano

Lori Feathers

Mary Ann Thompson-Frenk
& Joshua Frenk

Matthew Rittmayer

Meriwether Evans

Pixel and Texel

Nick Storch

Social Venture Partners Dallas

Stephen Bullock

## DONORS

Adam Rekerdres

Alan Shockley

Amrit Dhir

Anonymous (4)

Andrew Yorke

Anthony Messenger

Bob Appel

Bob & Katherine Penn

Brandon Childress

Brandon Kennedy

Caitlin Baker

Caroline Casey

Charles Dee Mitchell

Charley Mitcherson

Chilton Thomson

Cheryl Thompson

Christie Tull

Cone Johnson

CS Maynard

Cullen Schaar

Daniel J. Hale

Dori Boone-Costantino

Ed Nawotka

Elizabeth Gillette

Rev. Elizabeth
& Neil Moseley

Ester & Matt Harrison

Farley Houston

Garth Hallberg

Grace Kenney

Greg McConeghy

Jeff Waxman

JJ Italiano

Justin Childress

Kay Cattarulla

Kelly Falconer

Lea Courington

Leigh Ann Pike

Linda Nell Evans

Lissa Dunlay

Maaza Mengiste

Marian Schwartz
& Reid Minot

Mark Haber

Marlo D. Cruz Pagan

Mary Cline

Maynard Thomson

Michael Reklis

Mike Kaminsky

Mokhtar Ramadan

Nikki & Dennis Gibson

Olga Kislova

Patrick Kukucka

Patrick Kutcher

Richard Meyer

Sherry Perry

Steve Bullock

Suejean Kim

Susan Carp

Susan Ernst

Stephen Harding

Symphonic Source

Theater Jones

Thomas DiPiero

Tim Perttula

Tony Thomson

## SUBSCRIBERS

Ali Bolcakan

Amanda Harvey

Andre Habet

Andrew Bowles

Anita Tarar

Anonymous

Ben Fountain

Ben Nichols

Blair Bullock

Charles Dee Mitchell

Chris Sweet

Christie Tull

Courtney Sheedy

Daniel Galindo

David Tomlinson & Kathryn Berry

David Weinberger

Dawn Wilburn-Saboe

Elizabeth Johnson

Geoffrey Young

Holly LaFon

James Tierney

Jeffrey Collins

Jill Kelly

Joe Milazzo

John Schmerein

John Winkelman

Kevin Winter

Kimberly Alexander

Lesley Conzelman

M.J. Malooly

Margaret Terwey

Martha Gifford

Mary Brockson

Michael Elliott

Michael Filippone

Mies de Vries

Neal Chuang

Nhan Ho

Nicholas R. Theis

Patrick Shirak

Peter McCambridge

Rainer Schulte

Robert Keefe

Ronald Morton

Shelby Vincent

Suzanne Fischer

Sydney Mantrom

Tim Kindseth

Todd Jailer

Tom Bowden

Tracy Shapley

William Fletcher

William Pate

## FORTHCOMING FROM DEEP VELLUM

EDUARDO BERTI · *The Imagined Land*
translated by Charlotte Coombe · ARGENTINA

ALISA GANIEVA · *Bride & Groom*
translated by Carol Apollonio · RUSSIA

FOUAD LAROUI · *The Tribulations of the Last Sjilmassi*
translated by Emma Ramadan · MOROCCO

MARIA GABRIELA LLANSOL · *The Geography of Rebels Trilogy: The Book of Communities; The Remaining Life; In the House of July & August*
translated by Audrey Young · PORTUGAL

PABLO MARTÍN SÁNCHEZ · *The Anarchist Who Shared My Name*
translated by Jeff Diteman · SPAIN

BRICE MATTHIEUSSENT · *Revenge of the Translator*
translated by Emma Ramadan · FRANCE

SERGIO PITOL · *Mephisto's Waltz: Selected Short Stories*
translated by George Henson · MEXICO

SERGIO PITOL · *Carnival Triptych: The Love Parade; Taming the Divine Heron; Married Life*
translated by George Henson · MEXICO

ÓFEIGUR SIGURÐSSON · *Öræfi: The Wasteland*
translated by Lytton Smith · ICELAND

DEEP
VELLUM